I was jealous of them.

Already, I was jealous. They were at each other all the time, but I could see they also respected and, in a funny way, liked each other and liked to challenge and tease each other. I wanted them to like me, too. Who else would like me but these girls? I worried. I could count on the fingers of one hand the friends I had had and lately I had none. I felt like a leper because I saw the way some of the other kids looked at me in school and wherever else they saw me.

It's my own fault, I thought. My face might as well be made of glass and all my thoughts and memories printed on a screen inside my head that anyone could read.

My heart began to pound again. . . .

CAT

V.C. Andrews® Books

The Dollanganger Family Series:
Flowers in the Attic
Petals on the Wind
If There Be Thorns
Seeds of Yesterday
Garden of Shadows

The Landry Family Series:
Ruby
Pearl in the Mist
All That Glitters
Hidden Jewel
Tarnished Gold

The Casteel Family Series:
Heaven
Dark Angel
Fallen Hearts
Gates of Paradise
Web of Dreams

The Logan Family Series:
Melody
Heart Song
Unfinished Symphony
Music in the Night
Olivia

The Cutler Family Series:
Dawn
Secrets of the Morning
Twilight's Child
Midnight Whispers
Darkest Hour

The Orphans Miniseries:
Butterfly
Crystal
Brooke
Raven
Runaways

My Sweet Audrina (does not belong to a series)

The Wildflowers Miniseries:
Misty
Star
Jade
Cat

Published by POCKET BOOKS

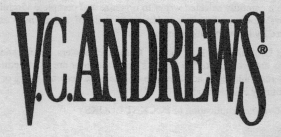

V.C. ANDREWS®

CAT

POCKET BOOKS
New York   London   Toronto   Sydney   Tokyo   Singapore

Following the death of Virginia Andrews, the Andrews family worked with a carefully selected writer to organize and complete Virginia Andrews' stories and to create additional novels, of which this is one, inspired by her storytelling genius.

This book is a work of fiction. Names, characters, places and incidents are products of the author's imagination or are used fictitiously. Any resemblance to actual events or locales or persons, living or dead, is entirely coincidental.

An *Original* Publication of POCKET BOOKS

POCKET BOOKS, a division of Simon & Schuster Inc.
1230 Avenue of the Americas, New York, NY 10020

Copyright © 1999 by the Vanda General Partnership

ISBN: 0-671-02803-0

First Pocket Books paperback printing October 1999

10 9 8 7 6 5 4 3 2 1

V.C. ANDREWS and VIRGINIA ANDREWS are registered trademarks of the Vanda General Partnership.

POCKET and colophon are registered trademarks of Simon & Schuster Inc.

Cover illustration by Lisa Falkenstern
Cover design by Tony Greco

Printed in the U.S.A.

CAT

Prologue

I woke with a terrible chill. I was shivering even before I opened my eyes. Cringing in bed, I drew my legs up tightly until my knees were against my stomach and I buried my face in the blanket, actually biting down on the soft, down comforter until I could taste the linen. No matter how warm my room was, I had to sleep with a blanket. I had to wrap myself securely or I couldn't sleep. Sometimes, during the night, I would toss it off, but by morning, it was spun around me again as if some invisible spider was trapping me in its web. I could feel the sticky threads on my fingers and feet, and struggle as much as I'd like, I was unable to tear myself free.

Exhausted, I lay there, waiting as the spider drew closer and closer until it was over me and I looked up into its face and saw that it was Daddy.

Prologue

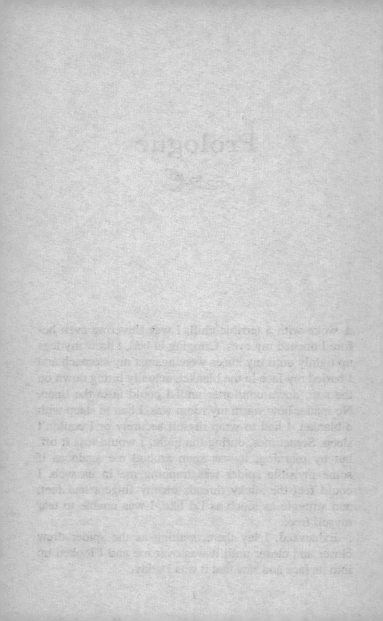

1

Because my daddy went to work so early, my mother was always the one left with the responsibility of waking me, if I didn't rise and shine on my own for school. She would usually wake me up by making extra noise outside my bedroom door. She rarely knocked and she almost never opened the door. I could probably count on the fingers of one hand how many times my mother had been in my bedroom while I was in it too, especially during the last five years.

Instead, she would wait for me to leave for school, and then she would enter like a hotel maid after the guests had gone and clean and arrange the room to her liking. I was never neat enough to please her, and when I was younger, if I dared to leave an undergarment on a chair or on the top of the dresser, she would complain vehemently and look like the wicked witch in *The Wizard of Oz*.

"Your things are very private and not for the eyes of others," she would scowl, and put her hands on me and shake me. "Do you understand, Cathy? Do you?"

I would nod quickly, but what others? I would wonder. My mother didn't like any of my father's friends or business associates and she had no friends of her own. She prized her solitude. No one came to our house for dinner very often, if at all, and certainly no one visited my room or came upstairs, and even if they had, they wouldn't see anything because Mother insisted I keep my door shut at all times. She taught me that from the moment I was able to do it myself.

Nevertheless, she would be absolutely furious now if I didn't put my soaps and lotions back in the bathroom cabinet, and once, when I had left a pair of my panties on the desk chair, she cut them up and spread the pieces over my pillow to make her point.

This morning she was especially loud. I heard her put down the pail on the floor roughly, practically slamming it. She was cleaning earlier than usual. The mop hit my door, swept the hard wood floor in the hallway and then hit my door again. I looked at the small clock housed in clear Danish crystal on my night table. The clock was a birthday present from my grandmother, my mother's mother, given only weeks before she had passed away from lung cancer. She was a heavy smoker. My grandfather was twelve years older than she was and died two years later from a heart attack. Like me, my mother had been an only child. Not long ago I found out I wasn't supposed to be, but that's another story, maybe even one that's more horrible than what's happened to me recently. Whatever, one thing was certain: we didn't have much family. Our Thanksgiving turkeys were always small. Mother didn't like leftovers. Daddy muttered that she threw away enough food to feed another family, but he never muttered loud enough for Mother to hear.

Part of the reason for our small Thanksgivings and Christmas holidays was because my father's parents had nothing to do with him or with us; his sister Agatha and his younger brother Nigel never came to see us either. My father had told me that none of his family members liked anyone else in the family and it was best for all of them to just avoid each other. It would be years before I would find out why. It was like finding pieces to a puzzle and putting them together to create an explanation for confusion.

When my mother hit the door with the mop again, I knew it was time to rise, but I was stalling. Today was my day at Doctor Marlowe's group therapy session. The other three girls, Misty, Star and Jade, had told their stories and now they wanted to hear mine. I knew they were afraid I wouldn't show up and to them it would be something of a betrayal. They had each been honest to the point of pain and I had listened and heard their most intimate stories. I knew they believed they had earned the right to hear mine, and I wasn't going to disagree with that, but at this very moment, I wasn't sure if I could actually gather enough courage to tell them my tale.

Mother wasn't very insistent about it. She had been told by other doctors and counselors that it was very important for me to be in therapy, but my mother didn't trust doctors. She was forty-six years old and from what I understood, she had not been to a doctor for more than thirty years. She didn't have to go to a doctor to give birth to me. I had been adopted. I didn't learn that until . . . until afterward, but it made sense. It was practically the only thing that did.

My chills finally stopped and I sat up slowly. I had a dark maple dresser with an oval mirror almost directly across from my bed so when I rose in the morning, the first thing I saw was myself. It was always a surprise to see that I had not changed during the night, that my face was still formed the same way (too round and full of baby fat), my eyes were still hazel and my hair was still a dull dark brown. In dreams I had oozed off my bones and dripped into the floor. Only a skeleton remained. I guess that signified my desire to completely disappear. At least that was what Doctor Marlowe suggested at an earlier session.

I slept in a rather heavy cotton nightgown, even during the summer. Mother wouldn't permit me to own anything flimsy and certainly not anything sheer. Daddy tried to buy me some more feminine nighties and even gave me one for a birthday present once, but my mother accidentally ruined it in the washing machine. I cried about it.

"Why," she would ask, "does a woman, especially a young girl or an unmarried woman, have to look attractive to go to sleep? It's not a social event. Pretty things aren't important for that; practical things are, and spending money on frilly, silly garments for sleep is a waste.

"It's also bad for sleep," she insisted, "to stir yourself up with narcissistic thoughts. You shouldn't dwell on your appearance just before you lay down to rest. It fills your head with nasty things," she assured me.

If my daddy heard her say these things, he would laugh and shake his head, but one look from her would send him fleeing to the safety and the silence of his books and newspapers, many of which she didn't approve.

When I was a little girl, I would sit and watch her look through magazines and shake her head and take a black magic marker to advertisements she thought were too suggestive or sexy. She was the stern censor, perusing all print materials, checking television programs, and even going through my schoolbooks to be sure nothing provocative was in them. She once cut illustrations out of my science text. Many times she phoned the school and had angry conversations with my teachers. She wrote letters to the administrators. I was always embarrassed about it, but I never dared say so.

Yawning and stretching as if I were sliding into my body, I finally slipped my feet into my fur-lined leather slippers and went into the bathroom to take a shower. I know I was moving much slower than usual. A part of me didn't want to leave the room, but that was one of the reasons I had been seeing Doctor Marlowe in the first place: my desire to withdraw and become even more of an introvert than I was before . . . before it all happened or, to be more accurate, before it was all revealed. When you can lie to yourself, you can hide behind a mask and go out into the world. You don't feel as naked nor as exposed.

I wasn't sure what I would wear today. Since it was my day in the center of the circle, I thought I should look better dressed, although Misty certainly didn't dress up for her day or any day thereafter. Still, I thought I might feel a little better about myself if I did. Unfortunately, my favorite dress was too tight around my shoulders and my chest. The only reason my mother hadn't cut it up for rags was she hadn't seen me in it for some time. What I chose instead was a one-piece, dark-brown cotton dress with an empire waist. It was the newest dress I had and looked the best on me even though my mother deliberately had bought it a size too big. Sometimes I think if she could cut a hole in a sheet and drape it over me, she'd be the happiest. I know why and there's nothing I can do about it except have an operation to reduce the size of my breasts, which she finds a constant embarrassment.

"Be careful to step on the sheets of newspaper," Mother warned when I opened my bedroom door to go down to breakfast. "The floor's still wet."

A path of old newspaper pages led to the top of the stairway where she waited with the pail in one hand, the mop, like a knight's lance, in the other. She turned and descended ahead of me, her small head bobbing on her rather long, stiff neck with every downward step.

The scent of heavy disinfectant rose from the hardwood slats and filled my nostrils, effectively smothering the small appetite I was able to manage. I held my breath and followed her. In the kitchen my bowl for cereal, my glass of orange juice and a plate for a slice of whole wheat toast with her homemade jam was set out. Mother took out the pitcher of milk and brought it to the table. Then, she looked at me with those large round dark critical eyes, drinking me in from head to foot. I was sure I appeared pale and tired and I wished I could put on a little makeup, especially after seeing how the other girls looked, but I knew Mother would make me wipe it off if I had any. As a general rule, she was against makeup, but she was especially critical of anyone who wore it during the daytime.

She didn't say anything, which meant she approved of my appearance. Silence meant approval in my house and there were many times when I welcomed it.

I sat and poured some cereal out of the box, adding in the blueberries and then some milk. She watched me drink my juice and dip my spoon into the cereal, mixing it all first. I could feel her hovering like a hawk. Her gaze shifted toward the chair my father used to sit on every morning, throwing daggers from her eyes as if he were still sitting there. He would read his paper, mumble about something, and then sip his coffee. Sometimes, when I looked at him, I found him staring at me with a small smile on his lips. Then he would look at my mother and turn his attention quickly back to the paper like a schoolboy caught peering at someone else's test answers.

"So today's your day?" Mother asked. She knew it was.

"Yes."

"What are you going to tell them?"

"I don't know," I said. I ate mechanically, the cereal feeling like it was getting stuck in my throat.

"You'll be blaming things on me, I suppose," she said. She had said it often.

"No, I won't."

"That's what that doctor would like you to do: put

the blame at my feet. It's convenient. It makes their job easier to find a scapegoat."

"She doesn't do that," I said.

"I don't see the value in this, exposing your private problems to strangers. I don't see the value at all," she said, shaking her head.

"Doctor Marlowe thinks it's good for us to share," I told her.

I knew Mother didn't like Doctor Marlowe, but I also knew she wouldn't have liked any psychiatrist. Mother lived by the adage, "Never air your dirty linen in public." To Mother, public meant anyone outside of this house. She had had to meet with Doctor Marlowe by herself, too. It was part of the therapy treatment for me and she had hated every minute of it. She complained about the prying questions and even the way Doctor Marlowe looked at her with what Mother said was a very judgmental gaze. Doctor Marlowe was good at keeping her face like a blank slate, so I knew whatever Mother saw in Doctor Marlowe's expression, she put there herself.

Doctor Marlowe had told me that it was only natural for my mother to blame herself or to believe other people blamed her. I did blame her, but I hadn't ever said that and wondered if I ever would.

"Remember, people like to gossip," Mother continued. "You don't give them anything to gossip about, hear, Cathy? You make sure you think about everything before you speak. Once a word is out, it's out. You've got to think of your thoughts as valuable rare birds caged up in here," she said pointing to her temple. "In the best and safest place of all, your own head. If she tries to make you tell something you don't want to tell, you just get yourself right up out of that chair and call me to come fetch you, hear?"

She paused, and birdlike, craned her long neck to peer at me to see if I was paying full attention. Her hands were on her hips. She had sharp hipbones that protruded and showed themselves under her housecoat whenever she pressed her palms into her sides. They looked like two pot handles. She was never a heavy woman, but all of this had made her sick, too, and she had lost weight until her cheeks looked flat and drooped like wet handkerchiefs on her bones.

"Yes, Mother," I said obediently, without looking up at her. When she was like this, I had trouble looking directly at her. She had eyes that could pierce the walls around my most secret thoughts. As her face had thinned, her eyes had become even larger, even more penetrating, seizing on the quickest look of hesitation to spot a lie.

And yet, I thought, she hadn't been able to do that to Daddy. Why not?

"Good," she said nodding. "Good."

She pursed her lips for a moment and widened her nostrils. All of her features were small. I remember my father once describing her as a woman with the bones of a sparrow, but despite her diminutive size, there was nothing really fragile about her, even now, even in her dark state of mind and troubled demeanor. Our family problems had made her strong and hard like an old raisin, something past its prime, although she didn't look old. There was barely a wrinkle in her face. She often pointed that out to emphasize the beneficial qualities of a good clean life, and why I shouldn't be swayed by other girls in school or things I saw on television and in magazines.

I laughed to myself thinking about Misty's mother's obsession with looking younger, going through plastic surgery, cosmetic creams, herbal treatments. Mother would put nothing more than Ivory soap and warm water on her skin. She never smoked, especially after what had happened to her mother. She never drank beer or wine or whiskey, and she never permitted herself to be in the sun too long.

My father smoked and drank, but never smoked in the house. Nevertheless, she would make a big thing out of the stink in his clothing and hang his suits out on her clothesline in the yard before she would permit them to be put back into the closet. Otherwise, she said, they would contaminate his other garments, and, "Who knows? Maybe the smell of smoke is just as dangerous to your health," she said.

As I ate my breakfast, Mother went about her business, cleaning the dishes from her own breakfast, and then she pounced on my emptied orange juice glass, grasping it in her long, bony fingers as if it might just sneak off the table and hide in a corner.

"Go up and brush your teeth," she commanded, "while I finish straightening up down here and then we'll get started. Something tells me I shouldn't be bringing you there today, but we'll see," she added. "We'll see."

She ran the water until it was almost too hot to touch and then she rinsed out my cereal bowl. Often, she made me feel like Typhoid Mary, a carrier of endless germs. If she could boil everything I or my father touched, she would.

I went upstairs, brushed my teeth, ran a brush through my hair a few times and then stood there, gazing at myself in the bathroom mirror. Despite what each of the girls had told me and the others about herself, I wondered how I could talk about my life with the same frankness. Up until now, only Doctor Marlowe and the judge and agent from the Child Protection Agency knew my story.

I could feel the trembling in my calves. It moved up my legs until it invaded my stomach, churned my food and shot up into my heart, making it pound.

"Come on if you're going," I heard Mother shout from below. "I have work to do today."

My breakfast revolted and I had to get to my knees at the toilet and heave. I tried to do it as quietly as I could so she wouldn't hear. Finally, I felt better and I washed my face quickly.

Mother had her light gray tweed short coat on over her housecoat and was standing impatiently at the front door. She wore her black shoes with thick heels and heavy nylon stockings that nearly reached her knees. This morning she decided to tie a light brown scarf around her neck. Her hair was the color of tarnished silver coins and tied with a thick rubber band in her usual tight knot at the base of her skull.

Despite her stern appearance, my mother had beautiful cerulean blue eyes. Sometimes I thought of them as prisoners because of the way they often caught the light and sparkled even though the rest of her face was glum. They looked like they belonged in a much younger woman's head, a head that craved fun and laughter. These eyes longed to smile. I used to think that it had to have been her eyes that had drawn my father to her, but that was before I learned about her having had inherited a trust when she turned twenty-one.

When my mother accused my father of marrying her for her money, he didn't deny it. Instead he lowered his newspaper and said, "So? It's worth ten times what it was then, isn't it? You should thank me."

Did he deliberately miss the point or was that always the point? I wondered.

I knew we had lots of money. My father was a stockbroker and it was true that he had done wonders with our investments, building a portfolio that cushioned us for a comfortable, worry-free life. Little did I or my mother realize just how important that would be.

Mother and I walked out to the car, which was in the driveway. My mother had backed it out of the garage very early this morning and washed the windshield as well as vacuumed the floor and seats. It wasn't a late-model car, but because of the way my mother kept it and the little driving she did, it looked nearly new.

"You're pale," she told me. "Maybe you should call in sick."

"I'm all right," I said. I could just hear them all saying, "We knew it. We knew she wouldn't come." Of course, they would be furious.

"I don't like it," Mother mumbled.

Every time she complained, it stirred the little frogs in my stomach and made them jump against my ribs. I got into the car quickly. She sat at the wheel, staring at the garage door. There was a dent in the corner where my father had backed into it one night with his car after he had had a little too much to drink with some old friends. He never repaired it and every time Mother looked at it, I knew she thought of him. It made the anger in her heart boil and bubble.

"I wonder where he is this fine morning," she said as she turned on the engine. "I hope he's in hell."

We backed out of the driveway and started away. My mother drove very slowly, always below the speed limit, which made drivers in cars behind us lean on their horns and curse through locked jaws of frustration.

Before my father had left, he had helped me get my permit and then my license, but Mother didn't like me driving. She thought the driving age should be raised to twenty-one, and even that was too low these days.

"People are not as mature as they were when I was younger," she told me. "It takes years and years to grow up and driving is a big responsibility. I know why your father let you do it," she added, grinding her teeth. She did that so often, it was a wonder she didn't have more dental problems. "Bribery," she spit. "Even hell is too good for him."

"It wasn't just bribery, Mother. I'm a careful driver," I said. She had yet to let me drive her car and had been in my father's car only twice when I had driven, complaining the whole time, each time.

"You can never be careful enough," she replied. These expressions and thoughts were practically automatic. I used to think Mother has tiny buttons in her brain and when something is said, it hits one of those buttons which triggers sentences already formed and ready to be sent out through her tongue. Each button was assigned a particular thought or philosophical statement.

This morning it was partly cloudy and a lot more humid than it had been the last few days. The weatherman predicted possible thunderstorms later in the afternoon. I could see some nasty looking clouds looming in the west over the ocean, waiting like some gathering army to launch an attack.

"I'll be home all day," Mother continued as we drove along. "If you need me, you don't hesitate to call, hear?"

"All right," I said.

"I've done all my food shopping. I've got to work on our books."

She meant our finances. My mother had gained control of most of that fortune and prided herself on how well she kept our accounts. She attacked it with the same degree of efficiency she attacked everything else. There was a button in her brain connected to "Waste not, want not."

When Doctor Marlowe's house came into view, Mother clicked her tongue and shook her head.

"I don't like this," she said. "I don't see any good coming from this."

I didn't speak. With obvious reluctance, she turned into the driveway and pulled up just as Jade's limousine was pulling away.

"Who is that spoiled girl?" she asked, her eyes narrowing as the limousine disappeared. She hoisted her shoulders and looked ready to pounce on my answer like some alley cat.

"Her name is Jade," I said. "Her father is an important architect and her mother manages sales for a big cosmetics company."

"Spoiled," she declared again with the rock solid firmness of a doctor pronouncing someone dead. She nodded and raised her eyes. "As ye sow, so shall ye reap."

She stopped the car and looked at me with eyes that always seemed to lay the blame totally at my feet, despite the way she would mutter about and curse my father.

"When will this be over?" she demanded, gazing so furiously at the house, I thought she might cause it to explode right before our eyes.

"I guess it'll be the same time as yesterday and the day before," I told her.

"Um," she said. She thought for a moment and then turned back to me sharply. "Remember, don't let that woman make you say anything you don't want to say," she warned.

"I won't."

She nodded, her eyes still fueled by fury, remaining as bright as two Christmas tree lights. Her lips stretched and she spoke through clenched teeth.

"I hope he's sitting in hell," she said.

I wondered why I didn't.

I should, I thought. I should hate him more than she does.

I gazed at the front door of Doctor Marlowe's house.

Maybe today, maybe today I would discover why all this was so.

It gave me the strength to open the door and step out.

Mother looked at me, shook her head, and drove away, her neck as stiff as ever. I watched her stop at the end of the driveway and then turn into the street and head back for home.

Then I took a very deep breath, pressed my clutched hands against my stomach, and walked up to the door to press the doorbell. When Doctor Marlowe's maid Sophie opened the door, I was surprised to see the three of them: Misty, Star and Jade, standing there right behind her, smiling, or more to the point, smirking out at me.

"We decided not to waste our time back there in Doctor Marlowe's office. If you didn't show up on schedule, we were all going to go home," Jade said, lifting the right corner of her mouth, and speaking in her most arrogant, haughty voice.

"I'm glad you came," Misty said with her habitually bubbly smile.

"Let's get started," Star added. She brought her hands to her hips and leaned toward me. "Well, c'mon in. Don't stand out there all day gaping at us like some dummy. Doctor Marlowe's waiting for you."

I stepped in and Misty jumped ahead of Sophie to quickly close the door.

"Gotcha," she said and laughed.

They gathered around me to march me back to Doctor Marlowe's office and for a few moments, I felt like I was going to my own execution.

There was plenty about myself I wanted to see die. Maybe, I thought, it was time to do it.

2

Doctor Marlowe was at her desk when we all marched into her office. She quickly finished whatever she was doing and joined us.

"Good morning, girls," she sang with that happy smile of welcome. "I didn't know anyone had arrived yet. Did you all come at the same time?"

"Where's Emma this morning?" Star asked, instead of answering her question. "She usually sets off the alarm when we appear."

Doctor Marlowe laughed. I admired her ability to never lose control, never get upset or angry at anything any of us said, especially Star, who never seemed to be tired of testing her. Of course, after having heard her story, I understood why Star was so angry all the time. And then I wondered if that wasn't really the way I should act, too.

"My sister had an early dental appointment. Everyone comfortable where you have been sitting?" she asked, glancing quickly at me. Now that I was actually here, she looked almost as nervous as I felt.

"Why shouldn't we be?" Star asked.

Doctor Marlowe's smile flickered like a flashlight with weakened batteries and then disappeared.

This morning she wore turquoise earrings and had a bit more of a wave in her dirty blond hair. It was trimmed neatly at her ears. As usual, she wore a skirt suit with a white silk blouse with pearl buttons closed at her throat.

The first time my mother had met her, she had seemed relieved that our therapist wasn't particularly pretty. For reasons I didn't quite understand, Mother was always suspicious of attractive women or else intimidated by them. There wasn't a movie star or a model with whom she didn't find fault. They were either obsessed with being too thin or conceited and had distorting priorities. Mother was proud of the fact that she rarely, if ever, looked in the mirror more than once or twice a day. She thought the world would be better without them and if she caught me gazing at myself, she would ask, "Why are you looking at yourself so much? If something's wrong, I'll tell you."

I didn't think I looked in the mirror any more than or even as much as girls my age did, but I couldn't help being self-critical and comparing myself to other girls and women I met. Doctor Marlowe's nose was a bit too long and her lips too thin, but she did have a figure I coveted. I would even like to be as tall. I always felt short and dumpy because of my own figure and height. Doctor Marlowe was at least six feet one and I was barely five feet four, and with my figure, that made me feel almost comical, distorted, despite the nice things Daddy used to say. He was practically the only one who tried to make me feel good about myself.

Was Mother right? Were those really all lies? And if they were, weren't there some lies we needed?

"Well, let's get started," Doctor Marlowe declared with a small clap. She nodded and sat and motioned for us to do the same.

There was a deep and long moment of silence, the kind that makes my heart stop and then pound. I could feel everyone's eyes on me. I actually began to tremble again, my thighs shaking. I embraced myself like someone who was afraid she would just fly apart.

"How are you all today?" Doctor Marlowe asked.

"Ginger peachy," Star said.

"Good," Misty said with a nice smile.

"I'd like to have slept in longer," Jade said. "It's supposed to be our summer holiday."

Doctor Marlowe laughed and gazed my way, her eyes soft, warm, compassionate.

Even so, a ribbon of pain stretched across my forehead from temple to temple, tightening and tightening until it felt like it was cutting through my brain.

"I think I woke up with a fever this morning," I said. "I had chills. I still have them a bit," I added and embraced myself. I rocked a little in my seat.

"Take it easy, Cathy," Doctor Marlowe said in a soft whisper. "Take deep breaths like you've done before."

I did so while the others continued to stare at me.

"I'm sorry," I whispered.

"Before I started to talk to all of you about my story, I felt like throwing up," Misty said in support.

"I did throw up this morning," I confessed.

Star frowned and shook her head.

"It's only us, Cat, not the whole country. You aren't on television on Oprah or something."

"Give her a chance," Jade ordered.

Star tilted her head a little and looked at Jade from an angle.

"Do you have some words of wisdom, Princess Jade?"

"I'm just saying it wasn't easy for any of us."

"I'm not saying it was," Star argued. "But whatever her story is, it can't be worse than any of ours, can it?"

Jade shrugged.

"I still haven't recovered from telling my own story," she said, as if we were all in a contest to outdo each other for misery.

The other two nodded in agreement.

"No one's going to laugh or anything," Misty promised with those sweet eyes.

All right, I thought. All right. They want to hear it. I'll tell them. I'll tell them everything. Then they'll be sorry. We'll all be sorry.

"My situation is a lot different from yours, and yours, and yours," I told each of them.

"How so?" Star fired back.

"For one thing, I'm adopted," I replied and quickly added, "but I didn't learn that until this year."

"Your parents kept that a secret all this time?" Misty immediately asked.

One thing about these girls, I thought, they weren't

CAT

going to be bashful about asking questions. It wasn't going to be easy hiding anything from them.

"Yes."

"Weren't there any baby pictures of you?" Jade asked.

"No. Well, not before I was two."

"Didn't you ever wonder about that? Everyone has pictures of their children when they were infants."

"No. I mean, I've wondered, but I didn't ask any questions about it."

"Why not?" Star demanded.

"I just didn't. It never occurred to me that I could be adopted. I look a little like my mother. We sort of have the same nose and mouth."

"Still, you could have asked about the pictures. What kind of parents wouldn't have pictures," Jade pursued.

"I don't like asking my mother questions," I admitted. "She doesn't like me to. She grew up believing children should be seen and not heard and that's how she wants me to be."

"You're not a child," Jade said.

"Hardly," Star added with a laugh. "One look at her will tell you that."

"I'm not just talking about her bosom," Jade snapped. "Some girls physically mature faster, but that doesn't make them grownups."

"I *was* mature very early," I admitted. Maybe I wanted to stop their bickering or maybe I just wanted to get my story out.

"How early?" Misty asked leaning toward me. "I mean, I'm still waiting."

Star and Jade laughed. Doctor Marlowe held her

23

lips still, but her eyes filled with a twinkle of amusement.

"I was still in the fourth grade when . . . when I started to develop."

"Fourth grade?" Star whistled. "You were wearing a bra in the fourth grade?"

"Not exactly. My mother didn't take me to buy a bra until I was in the sixth grade," I said.

"Well, what did you wear before then?" Star asked.

"She made me wear a sports bra, a size or so too small so it flattened me somewhat. It was made out of spandex and it felt like a straitjacket. It was really more for exercise, but she made me wear it all day. When I took it off at night, my chest was always sunburn red. I complained, but she said I had to do it because a bra for a girl my age would only emphasize my freakish appearance."

"Is that what she called it?" Jade said with a scowl. "Freakish?"

I nodded.

"I'd like to get a little more freakish myself then," Misty said. "I guess I'm going to end up having implants when I'm in my twenties."

"You shouldn't put so much emphasis on it just because men do," Jade said with fire in her eyes.

Misty gave her one of her small shrugs and turned back to me.

"What did your father say about it?" she asked.

"He didn't say anything to my mother right away. At least, not in front of me," I added. "My mother has always been more in charge when it came to matters concerning me, matters my father called 'girl stuff.' My father was always very busy. He's a stockbroker and he was out of the house early in the morning, except for weekends, of course."

"What's he look like?" Jade asked. "I mean, does he look like he could really be your father? Any resemblances?"

"I guess not. He's tall, six feet three and he's always been thin, no matter how much he ate or drank. He has very long hands. They're almost twice the size of mine, maybe three times, and his fingers . . ."

"What?" Misty asked.

I laughed.

"He used to play this game with me, itsy-bitsy spider."

"Huh?" Misty said.

"Don't you know it? You put the tips of your fingers together and you go, 'The itsy-bitsy spider crawled up the water spout. Down came the rain and washed the spider out. Out came the sun and dried up all the rain. And the itsy-bitsy spider crawled up the spout again,' " I recited and demonstrated, remembering. I guess I had a silly smile on my face. They all looked like they were going to break into hysterics at any moment.

"He used to do it with his fingers just like I showed you and then he would do it with his fingers on mine and he would crawl up and down my chest.

"I grew up thinking his fingers were really very much like spider legs, especially when he puts his hand on the table," I said remembering the image. "They look like two big spiders."

The three girls fixed their eyes on me and waited as pictures replaced pictures in my memory. I had my fingers on my chest and had turned them downward without even realizing what I was doing. My eyes closed and then snapped open and I felt myself return to the present.

"One of his fingers, the right forefinger, has a birthmark at the tip, a big, red blotch. It looks like he might have touched a hot stove or something. People who meet him for the first time sometimes ask if he had injured it and he shakes his head and holds it up like some sort of prize and explains it's just a birthmark.

"The palms of his hands are puffy and the lines are deep. In fact, he has a line so deep at the base of his left palm, it looks like he sliced it. He keeps his nails very trim. He gets manicures somewhere near his office once a week," I said. "He takes better care of his fingernails than my mother does of hers. I never saw her put nail polish on them. She's never had a manicure. Once, when I went over to a girlfriend's house and came home with my nails polished, she made me dip them in turpentine. I had to hold it in so long, it burned the skin on my fingers."

"Didn't she ever hear of nail polish remover?" Jade asked dryly. "My mother could get her a lifetime supply at cost."

"She's heard of it, but she doesn't own any. No nail polish, no need for nail polish remover," I said. I thought for a moment. "My father's nails shine. They're like ivory."

"How come you talk so much about your father's hands?" Misty asked with a wide smile.

I stared at her for a moment and then looked at Doctor Marlowe, whose eyes were narrowed and intense. How did we get into this so quickly? I wondered. Their questions had come at me like bullets. Maybe that was good. Maybe that was the best way, I thought.

I tried to swallow, but couldn't, and then I took a deep breath and felt like my father was squeezing my ribs and holding my lungs from expanding so I would keep all the secrets imprisoned in my heart. I took another deep breath to stop that all too familiar paralyzing numbness from gripping me.

"Drink some water," Doctor Marlowe ordered, jumping up and handing me a glass.

The girls all looked more frightened than surprised at my sudden reaction. They glanced at each other and then at the door as if they were considering running out of the room. They all looked sorry they had dragged me into my past so quickly. I laughed to myself.

You want to know why I think of my father's hands so much? Okay, I thought. You challenged me to tell you it all. Now you'll sit and listen even if it means you'll have nightmares too.

"Even though he worked very hard and spent a lot of time away from the house, at his firm or visiting with big clients, my father was the one who played with me. All the toys I had, I had because my father bought them. I can't remember my mother buying me any toys, not even a doll."

I shook my head and looked down.

"What?" Misty asked.

"I remember when he bought me a Barbie doll and my mother saw how it had breasts. She was so upset about it that she took the doll and smashed it to pieces with her rolling pin in the kitchen.

" 'This is disgusting!' she cried. 'How can they make

toys like this for children and how can you buy something like this for her?' she demanded of my father.

"My father shrugged and said the doll was the most popular toy in the store for girls. He said the stock in the company was a good one, too.

"I knew he was right, of course. Barbie dolls were very popular and I always wanted one and all the clothes, too. I had to settle for a rag doll my father brought home the next day. My mother inspected it closely and stamped her seal of approval on it when she saw there wasn't the slightest sexual thing about it. Despite the stringy hair, it didn't even look feminine. I ended up naming it Bones."

"Why didn't your father just tell her to stuff it?" Star asked.

"My father is a very quiet man. He doesn't raise his voice very often," I said.

"But he was just trying to let you be a normal girl. Your mother is a little extreme, don't you think?" Jade pursued.

"Why is your mother so bossy?" Misty asked.

Suddenly my heart started pounding and the blood rose to my face. I looked down when I spoke. It was almost as if I could see my life, my past and all the events being projected on the floor, the pictures flowing along in a continuous stream.

"My father's not a coward, even though I can't remember too many times when he and my mother shouted at each other," I said finally.

"That's practically all I *can* remember," Jade said.

"It's her day," Star said. "We already heard about you once and once is plenty."

"Is that so?" Jade countered.

"Yeah, it's so," Star said.

Jade stared darts back at her.

"Girls," Doctor Marlowe said softly, shaking her head. They both turned to me.

"That's not to say my mother didn't criticize my father," I continued. "I don't think a day went by when she didn't have some complaint about his drinking after work, the friends he had, the things she had asked him to do and he had forgotten or neglected. It was just that he would rarely . . . rarely challenge her. I used to believe that early in their marriage, my father decided the best thing for him to do was listen, nod, agree, accept and move on.

"Funny," I said smiling and still looking down, "but once I thought that he was wiser because of that. I had great respect for my father. He was a success in business and he seemed so well organized, contented, in control, I suppose is the word. He had an informed opinion about everything. Whenever he was challenged, he could explain his reasons and ideas. He was very good at convincing people. I guess that came from his being a stockbroker and having to sell hope.

"Dinner at our house was always educational. My father would comment about something that had happened in the government or in the economy, and most of the time, my mother and I would just listen. I mean, I would listen. When I looked at her, she seemed distracted, lost in her own thoughts. Yet, always at the end, she would say something like, 'Well, what do you expect, Howard? If you leave the barn doors open, the cows will get out.'"

"Huh?" Misty said. "What do cows have to do with it?"

I looked at her and smiled.

"My mother is full of old expressions like that. She has one for every occasion, every event."

"My granny has good expressions too," Star said.

"We already heard," Jade sang and threw her nauseatingly sweet smile at her. "It's Cat's day today, remember?" she said, enjoying her sweet taste of revenge.

Star smirked and then shook her head and laughed.

I was jealous of them. Already, I was jealous, I thought. They were at each other all the time, but I could see they also respected and in a funny way liked each other and liked to challenge and tease each other. I wanted them to like me too. Who else would like me but these girls? I worried. I could count on the fingers of one hand the friends I had had and lately, I had none. I felt like a leper because I saw the way some of the other kids looked at me in school.

It's my own fault, I thought. My face might as well be made of glass and all my thoughts and memories printed on a screen inside my head that anyone could see and read.

"I feel dirty," I muttered.

"What?" Misty asked. "Why?"

I looked up, not realizing I had spoken. It had just come out like a burp. My heart began to pound again. I glanced quickly, fearfully at Doctor Marlowe. She gave me her best calming expression.

"Did you say you feel dirty?" Misty asked.

"Let Cathy go at her own pace, Misty," Doctor Marlowe cautioned.

"She said it."

"I know. It takes time," Doctor Marlowe insisted, closing and opening her eyes softly. "You know that. All of you do," she added.

Misty relaxed and sat back.

After a few deep breaths, I went on.

"I guess I always felt people were looking at me all the time," I said.

"With a mother calling you a freak, why wouldn't you?" Jade muttered just loud enough for me to hear.

"Yes," I said. "I suppose that's true. My mother never liked me to wear what other kids my age were wearing. I had to always wear shoes, never sneakers, and my dresses were drab and not very fashionable. She complained often about the way other young people dressed to go to school, especially girls. Every time she brought me to school, she would wag her head and mutter about the clothes other kids wore. She wrote letters to the administration but for the most part, they went unanswered.

"One afternoon when she picked me up, she spotted a tiny spot of lipstick on my lip. I was in the fifth grade by then. A lot of girls came to school wearing lipstick, even though they were only ten years old. There was a girl named Dolores Potter who talked me into putting it on while we were in the girls' room together. I was embarrassed to admit I had never done it before, but she could tell and laughed because I put it on too heavily. I fixed it with a tissue and we went to class.

"I was so self-conscious about it. It was like I was

wearing a neon sign. I remember every time I lifted my eyes and gazed around the room, I was positive boys were looking at me more. When the bell rang for the end of the day, I rushed into the bathroom and wiped my mouth with a wet paper towel. I thought I had gotten it all off, but there was just this one spot in the corner.

"My mother always looks at me through a microscope. She doesn't look at anyone else that way. She fixes her eyes on me and looks at every little thing. If I have a strand of hair out of place or my collar is crooked, she spots it and makes me fix it. She has this thing about me being perfect, her idea of perfect," I added. "Anyway, she spotted the lipstick and erupted. The blood rose up through her face like lava. Her eyes popped and her eyebrows rose up and without a word, she brought her right hand around from the steering wheel and snapped it against the side of my face. It felt like a whip made of fire. She was so fast, too. I didn't have a chance to brace myself. My head nearly spun completely around. I guess it frightened me more than it actually hurt, but fear can slice through your heart and bring a deeper pain.

"I lifted my arms to protect myself. My mother could lose her temper and hit me a dozen times. Where she gets the strength for someone her size, I don't know, but she sure can explode."

"You mean she still hits you?" Jade asked.

"Sometimes. Usually, it's just a slap; she doesn't hit me hard anymore and always only once."

"Whoopie do," Jade said. "How lucky can you be?"

"Next time she goes to slap you, put your fist right in her face," Star advised.

"I couldn't do that. My mother just believes if you spare the rod, you spoil the child."

"You're not a child!" Jade practically yelled at me. She looked at Doctor Marlowe. "The girl's seventeen, isn't she?" Her eyes were bright with anger, like sparklers on July Fourth. "That's the trouble with parents these days. They don't know when to stop treating us like children."

"Amen to that," Star said.

"It's not easy for my mother," I said in her defense. "The entire burden of raising me has fallen on her shoulders. She doesn't have any family support system. It's really just the two of us," I explained. "I try to be like she wants me to be. I try not to make her any unhappier."

I looked at Doctor Marlowe because she and I had discussed some of this. She nodded slightly.

"I mean, my mother is a victim, too. She doesn't mean to be cruel or anything. She's just . . ."

"What?" Misty asked.

"Frightened," I said.

Doctor Marlowe's eyes filled with satisfaction and she relaxed her lips into a soft smile.

"It took me a long time to understand that, to realize it," I said, "but it's true. We're two mice living alone in a world full of predatory cats and lots of traps."

"Is that another one of her expressions?" Jade asked.

"No. It's one of mine," I said. She shook her head and looked away.

"Did your father hit you, too?" Misty asked.

"No," I said. "He never touched me in a way that wasn't affectionate or loving," I added.

I glanced at Doctor Marlowe. Should I say it now? Should I begin to talk about the deeper pain? Should I start to explain how those fingers burned through me and touched me in places I was afraid to touch myself?

Should I talk about lips that had become full of thorns? Should I describe the screams I heard in the night, screams that woke me and confused me until I realized they were coming from inside me? Is it time to bid the little girl inside me good-bye forever and ever?

In my dreams Doctor Marlowe was standing off to the side with a stopwatch in her hand. I was bracing to begin my flight. Seconds ticked away. She looked up at me almost as she was looking at me now. Her thumb was on the watch's button.

"Get ready, Cathy. Get set."

"What if my legs don't move?"

"They will; they must. It's time. Five, four, three . . ."

She pushed down on the button and shouted, "Go! Go on, Cathy. Get out of here. Hurry. Run, Cathy. Run!"

I let go of the little hand that I held and charged forward, tears streaming down my face. I looked back only once to see a rag doll staring after me. It was Bones, but its face had become Daddy's face.

I ran faster and faster and harder and harder until I was here in Doctor Marlowe's office, surrounded by my sisters in pain.

3

"**M**others can be a lot tougher than fathers," Misty was saying. "And a lot meaner."

"What?"

I didn't really hear her. It was as if she were standing behind a glass wall and her voice was muted.

"Mothers can't hit as hard, but they can sting more with their words and their looks sometimes," she explained with a nod. She looked at Jade and Star, who just stared at her. Then, looking as if she was going to start to cry, she sat back in her chair.

"Anyway," I began again so *I* wouldn't cry, "after the lipstick incident, my mother decided to take me out of public school and enroll me in a parochial school."

"Just because of that little bit of lipstick?" Jade cried.

"I wasn't that unhappy about it," I said quickly. "I had to wear a uniform and that ended my feeling so

35

different from the other girls because of the clothing my mother insisted I wear. No one was permitted to put on any makeup, of course, even lipstick, which made my mother happy. Discipline was strict. I knew girls, however, who snuck cigarettes in and smoked them. One was caught and expelled immediately and that stopped the smoking for a while. I got into trouble with Sister Margaret, who was basically the disciplinarian, because I went into the girls' room when two girls were smoking and the smell got into my clothes."

"So why would that get you into trouble?" Star asked.

"Sister Margaret is known for her nose, not because it's too big or anything, but because she can smell cigarette smoke a mile away. Her nostrils twitch like a rabbit's when she suspects someone.

"Anyway, later I was in the cafeteria waiting to get my lunch. I wasn't even thinking about having been in the bathroom with the smokers when suddenly I felt her hand squeeze down on my left shoulder, her fingers pinching me hard and pulling me out of the line.

" 'Come with me,' she demanded, and marched me to the office where she accused me of smoking just because she could smell it in my hair and clothes. I swore I hadn't been smoking and I started to cry, which was enough for Sister Louise, the principal, to judge me innocent, but Sister Margaret was relentless.

" 'All right, if you didn't smoke, you were right in it and certainly close enough to see what was going on. Who was smoking?' she demanded.

"The thought of telling on girls I had just gotten to know was terrifying, almost as terrifying as being caught myself. I shook my head and she grabbed my shoulders and shook me so hard, I thought my eyes would roll out. The sisters could hit you, too," I told them.

In anticipation of what I was about to describe, Star's eyes widened with anger.

"She made me put out my hands and slapped them with a ruler until the tears were streaming down my cheeks and my palms were nearly cherry red and I couldn't close my fingers."

"I'd have kicked her into her precious heaven," Star said.

"What did you do?" Misty asked.

"I told her again and again I didn't know who was smoking. 'I don't know everyone,' I lied. I closed my eyes expecting lightning to strike me or something because I was lying to a nun.

" 'Then you'll point them out,' she decided and marched me back to the cafeteria.

"The moment we entered, all the girls knew why I had been brought back. They stopped talking and looked up at me. You could almost hear them breathe. The two girls who had been smoking were very frightened. They looked down quickly, probably reciting Hail Marys at the table.

" 'They're not here,' I said.

" 'What do you mean? They have to be here. Everyone's here,' Sister Margaret snapped. She still had her hand on my shoulder and squeezed so hard, it sent pain down my spine and through my legs.

"I pretended to look around the cafeteria and then I shook my head.

V. C. ANDREWS

" 'They're not here!' I cried. Tears were dripping off my chin by now.

"She was fuming. I thought I could see the smoke she hated so much coming out of her ears.

" 'Very well,' she said. 'Until your memory improves, you'll eat lunch by yourself in my office facing the blank wall every day.' She kept me there for a week before telling me to return to the cafeteria. The good thing was they never told my mother," I said.

"How old were you when this all happened?" Jade asked.

"I had just turned eleven. I was still in the fifth grade."

"Girls were smoking in the fifth grade?" she muttered.

"That's nothing. Kids in my school have been smoking forever," Star added.

"Terrific. Maybe Cathy's mother is right. Maybe the country is going to hell," Jade said.

"You don't know anything about hell," Star told her. "Your idea of hell is a bad hairdo."

"Is that so?"

"Girls. Aren't we getting a little off course?" Doctor Marlowe softly suggested.

Jade threw a look at Star that could stop a charging bull, but Star waved it off with a smug turn of her head and a small grunt.

"It sounds so horrible. What did your father say about your changing to a parochial school?" Misty asked. "Was he for it, too?"

"Like I said, when it came to most things concerning me, my mother was in charge. She told him what she

38

wanted me to do, of course. It was an expense, but he just nodded as usual, glanced at me for a moment, snapped his paper and continued to read."

"Didn't he care about what you thought and wanted?" Misty followed.

I shook my head.

"Another absentee parent," Jade quipped. "Why do they bother to have children in the first place? What are we, some kind of status symbol, something to collect like a car or a big-screen television set? I'm not going to have any children unless my husband signs a contract in blood, swearing to be a concerned parent."

"You know you have to get pregnant to have children," Star teased with a coy smile. "You know that means you'll lose your perfect figure, and you'll throw up in the morning."

"I know what it is to be pregnant, thank you."

"Unless you adopt like her parents did," Star said nodding at me.

"Yes, that's right," Misty said. "It doesn't sound like they really wanted children. Why did they adopt you?" she wondered.

I turned and gazed through the window. Angry clouds had reached Brentwood and had drawn a dark gray veil over the trees, the grass and flowers. The wind was picking up and the tree branches were swaying. They looked like they were all saying, "No, no, no."

Why did they adopt me? If I had asked myself this question once, I had asked it a thousand times. My mother wouldn't reveal any answers, but I had my own deep suspicions, suspicions I had never expressed before, even to Doctor Marlowe. When I glanced at her, I thought she was hoping I would now and I thought maybe this was one reason she wanted me in this group therapy.

"I can't imagine, could never imagine my mother having a baby the normal way," I began. "I have seen my father kiss her on the forehead and occasionally on the cheek, but I have never seen them kiss like people in love, never on the lips. Mother probably would be thinking of some contagious disease if he did. Even when he kissed her on the forehead, she would turn away and wipe it off with the back of her hand. Sometimes, he saw her do it; sometimes he didn't."

"Don't they sleep together?" Star asked.

"Not in the same bed," I said. "They always had twin beds separated by a nightstand. He's not there anymore, of course."

"But even people who don't spend the night in the same bed can get together long enough to make a baby," Jade said. "I have friends whose parents even have separate bedrooms."

"What do they do, make a date to have sex?" Star asked her.

"I don't know. Maybe," Jade replied, thoughtful for a moment. She smiled. "Maybe it's more romantic."

"Oh yeah, you're married, but you got to make a date to have sex. That's really romantic."

"Passion should be . . . unexpected," Misty said with dreamy eyes turned toward the ceiling. "You've got to turn toward the man you love and have your eyes meet and then float into each other's arms with music in your heart."

"You're living in your own soap opera," Star told her, but not with her usual firmness. She looked like she hoped she was wrong.

"Maybe, but that's the way it's going to be for me and the man who loves me," Misty insisted.

Jade drew her lips up in the corners and shook her head. Then she turned back to me.

"So you don't think your mother and father had sex? Is that what you're saying?"

"They had to have had it once," I said.

"What do you mean? You just said they adopted you."

"My father told me there was almost a baby. He was alone with me one night when I was feeling very low, and he told me the story. He said my mother didn't know she was pregnant or didn't want to know. She found out when she had a bad pain in her stomach, went to the bathroom and lost the baby that was in her. She flushed it down the toilet."

"Ugh," Misty said.

"She collapsed and he had to help her to bed. She refused to go to a doctor even though she kept bleeding. My father made it sound as if she wanted it to happen. From the way he described it to me, I don't think she wanted to have sex and I think she was angry it had happened and she had become pregnant. I don't know. To this day I can't imagine them making love," I said. I guess I had a guilty look on my face. Misty widened her eyes a little and leaned toward me.

"What?" she whispered.

"Nothing," I said quickly and looked away. My heart had started racing again, beating almost like a wild frantic animal in my chest.

"Come on. We've told you lots of things we wouldn't dare tell anyone else," she urged.

"You know that's true, Cat," Star said. "We hardly have a secret left."

"You can trust us," Misty said. "Really. Who are we to talk about someone else, right?"

I looked back at the three of them. They did look sincere.

My mother's warning returned, but she didn't understand how important it was for me to get all this out. Look what keeping the ugliness inside her had done to her, I thought. I don't want that to happen to me.

"After my father had told me the story of the lost baby, I would spy on them," I confessed and quickly added, "I was just very curious."

"So? What did you see?" Star followed.

"How did you spy on them?" Misty asked.

"All our bedrooms are upstairs, next to each other. We have a two-story Spanish colonial with a deck running alongside their bedroom and mine."

"A Monterey-style cantilevered porch, probably," Jade said knowingly. "My father designed a house like that and I saw the drawings," she explained.

"Thanks for the information," Star said. "I couldn't have lived ten more minutes without it."

"If you don't want to learn anything . . ."

"Let her talk!" Misty exclaimed, excited and anxious for me to continue. "Go ahead, Cat," she urged. "I'm listening even if they're not."

"Usually, when they were both in their bedroom, I would hear some muffled conversation for a few minutes and then silence. I couldn't help thinking about it. I had read some things, knew some things."

"So you went out on the porch and peeked in their window?" Star asked impatiently.

"Yes, but only a few times," I added.

"And?" she asked, holding up her arms in anticipation.

"My mother sleeps in a nightgown with a cotton robe wrapped around her. Every time I looked in, she had her back to my father and he had his back to her. I never saw them embrace each other or touch each other or even kiss each other. I remember thinking they were like two strangers sharing a room for the night. How could they ever have made a baby?"

"No wonder they broke up. I'm surprised they were together as long as they were," Star said. Misty and Jade nodded.

"So your mother had gotten pregnant against her will, didn't want to have sex with your father anymore, and therefore, the only way they would ever have any children was by adopting," Jade concluded.

"Maybe someone else had made her pregnant," Star conjectured.

"No, I doubt that," I said.

"Maybe your father practically raped her," Misty suggested, "and that was why she wanted to lose the baby."

"You ought to write soap operas," Star told her.

Misty shrugged and motioned for me to continue.

"Why would her father remain married if he had no love life?" Jade pondered.

"Maybe there's something wrong with her father now. Maybe he's one of those men who can't have sex

43

anymore," Star suggested. "I heard that can happen to a man. He's impotent or something," she added, insecure about the word.

"No," I said, a little too fast.

"What do you mean, no? How do you know? Have you seen him with some other woman? Is that why they got divorced?"

"That's it, isn't it?" Misty asked, smiling. "Welcome to the club."

I looked away again, took a deep breath, and then looked at them and shook my head.

"No, I never saw him with anyone else."

"So then, how can you be so sure?" Star queried. She turned her eyes on me like two tiny knives. What she saw in mine made her eyes widen as she continued to look at me.

"I know what she's saying," she said almost in a whisper.

They were all staring now, a cold look of realization moving in a wave from one face to the other, and with it, an explosion of pity, fear and disgust in their eyes.

It felt like all the blood in my body was rising and gathering at my throat. Suddenly, I couldn't swallow, but I couldn't breathe either. I guess I was getting whiter and whiter. Doctor Marlowe's face erupted into a look of serious concern. She rose from her chair.

"Let's give Cathy a short break," she suggested. "Come on, honey. I want you to splash your face in cold water and relax for a few moments."

I felt her helping me to my feet, but I wasn't sure they wouldn't just turn to air and let the rest of me fold to the floor. Like a sleepwalker, I followed Doctor Marlowe out to the bathroom and did what she prescribed. The cold water revived me. The blood retreated and I could swallow again and breathe.

"Feeling better?" she asked.

I nodded.

"You don't have to continue, Cathy. Maybe I'm rushing you," she suggested.

I considered it. How comfortable and easy it would be for me to agree and go home, return to my room and go to bed. I could pull the blanket up to my chin and shut my eyes and squeeze my legs against my stomach and wait for sleep to open a door into a happy place, someplace where I could just drift, float on warm clouds and forget and forget and forget.

But another part of me wanted to come out, to leave the room and be in the real world again. How would I ever get back to the real world if I just ran home?

"No," I said. "I want to keep trying."

"You sure, honey?" she asked.

I looked at my face in the mirror. It was still a mask. I was tired of looking at it. It was time to tear it off and take a chance on what I would find. Would I find a little girl again? Had all that had happened stopped me from growing up? How silly that would be, a little girl's face on a body as mature as mine.

Or would I simply find a shattered face, cracked like some piece of thin china, the lines running down from my eyes where tears had streaked over my cheeks and chin. How long would it take to mend that face? Would it ever be mended so that the cracks would disappear and not look like scars of sadness?

Was I pretty? Could I ever be pretty? Did I have a

face that someone could love under this mask? Could I ever want to be kissed and touched? Could I dream and fantasize like Misty just had and find myself in a romantic place?

Daddy used to tell me so. He would cup my face in his hands and kiss the tip of my nose and say I was blossoming and soon all of my mirrors would reflect my beauty. When he spoke to me like that, I felt I was in a fairy tale and maybe I could be someone's princess. For a long time, he made me feel like I was his special princess, but because of that had my ability to love someone been crushed like a small flower, smashed into the earth, fading, fading, dying away like some distant star given a moment to twinkle before it fell back into the darkness forever and ever?

No, I didn't want to go home again. I had to keep trying.

"I'll go back," I insisted.

"Okay," Doctor Marlowe said, "but if you change your mind or have any problems, please don't hesitate to stop and ask to go home. I don't want to lose all the progress we've made to date. That can happen if things are rushed sometimes," she said.

"Rushed?" I laughed and the sound of that laughter seemed strange even to me. I knew it was strange and worrisome because Doctor Marlowe didn't smile but grimaced instead.

"Rushed? You know what it's like to look out the car window and see girls my age and younger walking on the sidewalk with their friends and boyfriends, their faces full of joy, their lives full of promises? I feel like an animal in a cage. I didn't put myself into that cage, either. It's not fair. I want to get out, Doctor Marlowe."

"I know, honey, and I'm going to help you do just that."

I gazed at the bathroom door.

"They all had bad times, too, but they looked so shocked and afraid back there."

She nodded.

"One or two of them might not want to stay, but somehow, I think you'll all get through it," she said. She squeezed my hand and I took a deep breath and smiled. "Ready?"

"Yes. Take me back. I want to focus on all the bad things just like you told me to do, and I want to put all my anger and strength into smashing them to bits forever and ever. Will I ever be able to do that?"

She smiled.

"I know you will," she said firmly enough to make me feel confident.

I walked out and returned to the office. I could see they had been talking incessantly about me. The expressions on their faces were so different, the hardness gone from Star, the smugness gone from Jade, and the innocence gone from Misty. We were doing what Doctor Marlowe had intended: we were changing each other as we changed ourselves. Like sisters related not through blood but through adversity and turmoil, we gathered around each other and warmed each other with our mutual pain and fear.

Together, we would help each other kill the demons.

I was anxious to go on.

4

Their eyes were full of many new questions now, questions I was still answering myself. How could all that have happened to me and right under my mother's eyes, too? How is a garden prepared and cultivated to grow black flowers full of thorns and poison? That was where I had found myself planted.

They waited patiently for me to sit and gather my thoughts. I took a small breath and began.

"When I was very little nothing seemed as important to my mother as my being able to care for myself. I was only three when she insisted I dress myself. She taught me how to run my own bath and I was given the responsibility to undress, clean and dress myself without her help. She would put out the clothes I was to wear, but she didn't stand around to help me put them on. If I didn't put something on correctly, she sent me back to my room to do it right.

"Personal hygiene, being in charge of my own body, was the most important thing to her. It was more important than anything else, school, manners, anything.

"It was hard when I got sick. I remember times when I threw up and she made me undress myself, bathe and dress myself even though I was nauseous and had cramps. I cried out for her, but she would stand outside the door and give me directions, insisting that I learn to guard and protect myself. To be naked in front of anyone, even my parents, was to be avoided at all costs."

"That's sick," Jade said. "Why would she make her own child ashamed of herself?"

"My mother doesn't think of it that way," I explained. "She thinks you should be ashamed only if someone else looks upon you. Your body is holy, precious, very private."

"No wonder your parents rarely had sex," Star muttered."

"My mother doesn't even go to the doctor because of the way she thinks," I revealed. "She's never had a gynecologist examine her and she hates taking me to any doctors. Whenever I was sick, she would try all her old-fashioned remedies first and take me only if they failed."

"Not getting herself regular checkups is so stupid," Jade said. "She could get cancer or something she might have prevented."

"What does she do when she's so sick that her remedies don't help?" Misty asked.

"I don't remember her ever being very sick. She's had colds, but she's in good health, I guess, although lately, she occasionally loses her breath and has to sit for a while almost immediately after she begins to clean. She says it's because of all that's happened and in time, it will pass.

"Anyway, I grew up with her ideas rolling around in my head like marbles pounding every time someone saw an uncovered part of me. It was especially hard in physical education class, dressing in the locker room. I never ever took a shower in school, not even in parochial school where we had individual showers."

"What did you expect would happen if someone saw you naked?" Star asked.

"I don't know. It just . . . sent a chill through me when it happened. I even imagined my mother standing there looking upset."

"You're going to grow up like her, a weirdo," Star threatened.

"No, she won't," Doctor Marlowe insisted. She turned to Star. "None of you will be weird."

"You mean weirder, don't you?" Jade said. "It's already too late to stop weird."

They all laughed. I felt a little better, stronger. I can do this, I chanted, trying to encourage myself. I can. I must face the demons and destroy them or Star will be right.

I paused, looked down, thought about how I would continue and then looked up at them.

"My father didn't have the same ideas about it all," I said, "although he behaved in the same way he did with everything else, which means he didn't argue with my mother about it. Right from the beginning, he pretended it was going to be our little secret, our special secret."

"What was?" Misty said almost before the words were out of my mouth. She grimaced with confusion.

"Give her a chance," Jade chastised.

"Yeah, stop rushing her," Star ordered.

"I'm sorry. I'm sorry."

It struck me funny how they were all becoming as protective as Doctor Marlowe.

"It's all right. I know it's hard to understand," I said, offering Misty a small smile. "I already told you that my father didn't have much to do with raising me. I rarely went anywhere with him without my mother along. He almost never attended any program at school that I participated in. He always went to bed early because he was up for the stock market so early. We didn't spend all that much time together in the evening. By the time we finished dinner and I did my homework, he was often on his way to bed. That was the routine year round."

"Didn't you ever go on a family trip or a vacation?" Jade asked.

"No, not really. A day's travel was it. My mother doesn't like to sleep in a strange bed. She says hotel rooms are never cleaned well enough and you're always sleeping in someone else's dirt.

"I recall a few times when my father went somewhere by himself, but my mother didn't seem to mind that. Then, there was a time when he took me," I said.

They all looked like they were holding their breath, but I wasn't ready to talk about that yet. I closed my eyes. It looked like red webs were spun on the underside of my eyelids.

"When I was little and left on my own to bathe and

51

dress myself, my father would sometimes appear. That was the secret. He made it clear that I shouldn't tell my mother. We both knew she wouldn't like it and my father said we shouldn't make her unhappy. She works too hard for both of us, he explained.

"She didn't see him go into your room?" Misty asked.

"She was usually downstairs preparing breakfast or dinner or cleaning up at the time. Mother has always been so precise about what she does. She keeps to her schedule no matter what," I explained. "I almost know to the minute where she'll be and what she'll be doing. Being organized makes her comfortable.

"Even though it is so long ago, I can clearly remember the first time my daddy came into my bathroom. I was already in the tub. I didn't hear him enter the bedroom. I think he must have been practically tiptoeing. He gazed in at me and smiled and asked me if I was all right.

"I nodded and he felt the water, dipped his right forefinger in like a thermometer and wiggled it in the air, that birthmark bright.

" 'Good,' he said with a big smile, 'it's not too hot.'

"He brushed his hand over my hair and then knelt beside the tub and asked me to show him how I washed myself.

"I was always eager for him to pay more attention to me. I wanted him to hold me and hug me and kiss me. He was my daddy and I looked to him often, anticipating some warm words, some gentle touch, some loving smile. That was all so rare in my house, so when he did this, I was very happy. I mean, that's why I wasn't afraid or . . ."

"You don't have to do that," Doctor Marlowe said softly. They all turned to her, but she didn't explain.

She didn't have to explain it to me. I knew what she meant. She wanted me to stop blaming myself, stop making excuses. I nodded. When I turned back to the girls, they looked even more intrigued.

" 'I know your mother has taught you how important it is to be clean all over,' he said. 'Go on. Let me see how you do it.'

"You can't imagine how excited I was to perform for him. I scrubbed my elbows and my little legs. I washed my neck vigorously, especially behind my ears, and then I stood up and washed between my legs and behind.

"He laughed and clapped and then he left and I felt so happy about it, but when I saw him later, he looked at my mother and then back to me and winked. In front of her he tried not to act so interested in me. He practically ignored me. When I tried to cuddle up beside him on the sofa, he told me I should go to sleep and I remember feeling as if I had been slapped even though he merely lifted his eyes and shook his head. Then he went back to what he was reading.

"The only time he really showed interest in me, smiled and laughed and touched me lovingly was when he visited me in the bathroom while I took my bath and that was only occasionally at best.

"Until . . ."

"What?" Misty practically jumped to ask.

"The bumps."

"Bumps?"

"She means until her breasts started to form," Jade said with narrow, sharp eyes. She glanced at Star who nodded and then turned back to me. "Right?"

"Yes," I said. My eyes burned with tears that welled behind my lids. I swallowed back the small scream that wanted so much to come rushing out of my mouth. "Yes," I whispered, not even sure if I had said it.

"Oh," Misty said, her lips in a small circle, her eyes bright with understanding, but shock as well.

"I don't know how it was for the rest of you, but when it began to happen to me, I was frightened. I told my mother about it and she told me to stop talking nonsense.

" 'It's not nonsense, Mother. It's really happening to me!' I protested one morning at breakfast.

"My father put down his paper and looked at me with surprise, too, but he didn't say anything to help me. He just looked a little interested and then he went back to his paper.

" 'You're too young for such a thing,' my mother said throwing me a hard look. 'Girls today rush everything. You're imagining it.'

" 'No, I'm not,' I cried, tears now building in my eyes. 'I'll show you.'

"I started to unbutton my blouse and she screamed so loud and shrilly, I felt like she had sent a lightning bolt through my body. I remember I literally froze, terrified of even moving my fingers.

" 'Take it easy, Geraldine,' my father said. 'She doesn't understand.'

"I guess she realized how dramatic and horrifying she was. She became calmer and lectured me softly.

" 'We don't disrobe in any other room of the house but our bedrooms and our bathrooms,' she explained.

" 'I'll go up to my bathroom to show you,' I offered.

" 'This isn't the time for that. It's breakfast time and you're off to school. Put this nonsense out of your mind,' she insisted.

"I gazed at my father, hoping he would speak up again, but he just shook his head at me and went back to what he was reading.

"I tried to bring it up again with my mother when I returned from school, but again, she refused to listen. She insisted it was all part of my confused imagination.

" 'They make sex such a big thing on television and in movies and books today that it infects children,' she orated. She could step up on a soapbox at a moment's notice and deliver a speech about the disgusting immorality alive in the world. She didn't accidentally use the word 'infects,' by the way. My mother thinks of it as a disease, almost something you can catch by breathing near promiscuous people. She had me thinking that way. I remember holding my breath or covering my mouth when classmates said or did things I knew my mother would disapprove of."

All three girls had their mouths slightly open, their eyes wide as they listened and gazed at me with astonishment.

"I know how stupid that sounds now, but that's the way I thought.

"Anyway, a few nights later, I heard Daddy enter my bedroom and come to the door of my bathroom while I was taking my bath. As I told you before, I was about nine years old at the time which was why I was nervous and confused. My body seemed to be racing ahead. Maybe I was freakish.

" 'So what's this you've been trying to tell your mother?' he asked as he approached.

"I sat up to show him and he nodded. He studied me like a doctor for a moment and then he pressed my chest softly with those spider leg fingers.

" 'Looks like you're right,' he said nodding and smiling. 'I'll speak to your mother about it. Don't be afraid,' he told me. 'It's earlier than most girls, but it's nothing bad, nothing to be afraid to see happening.'

"He spoke so gently, so kindly, I felt relieved. Why couldn't my mother be this kind, this concerned and loving? I wondered.

" 'I can tell you're going to be a very pretty girl, a special girl,' he continued. 'Daddy's special girl,' he added. He had never said that to me before. I was very happy about it. If this would make him love me even more, I thought, then it must be good.

"A little less than a week afterward, my mother came to my bedroom door while I was doing homework. She entered and closed it behind her.

" 'All right,' she said stretching and tightening her lips until they were two pale red thin lines over her chin, 'let me see what you're talking about.'

"I just imagined my father had done what he had promised and spoken to her about it. No longer afraid or ashamed, I got up and unbuttoned my blouse to show her. She looked at me, but unlike my father, she looked disgusted by it. She had such an unpleasant expression on her face, I thought there really was something wrong with me.

" 'Is it all right?' I asked her, my voice shaking with some panic.

" 'No,' she said. 'It's far too soon. I don't like how it shows under your blouse either. I'll get something proper for you to wear tomorrow,' she promised, turned and left me standing there feeling hideous.

"The next day she bought me a sports bra, but my development continued at an accelerated pace. By the time the school year ended, I had a distinct bosom. I even had cleavage," I said.

"That's so unfair," Misty moaned. "My mother wants to buy me a Wonder Bra and here you had cleavage in the fifth grade!"

"Despite my development, my mother fought buying me a regular bra. I complained about the sports bra and she replaced it with a little bigger size, but it still pinched and squeezed. It was such a relief to get undressed every night.

"My mother wouldn't listen to any complaints. She told me to work on putting my mind off it. If I told her about a tingle or a feeling I could describe only as a tickle, she would turn crimson and scream at me for not keeping such thoughts buried in my mind. Once, she even slapped me because I mentioned it in front of my father. Then she pulled me aside and said, 'There are things decent women don't mention in front of men, ever. Hear?'

"Men? I thought. My father was a man, of course, but I didn't lump him in with other men. I remember feeling so strange about the way she had referred to him. Almost as if he were the enemy. We had to hide things from him, too, just because he was a man. What would happen if she knew my daddy's and my secret? I wondered. Daddy looked worried for a moment and then smiled when he realized I had kept it our little secret.

"Of course, I nodded after everything my mother told me and I tried to behave as she wanted me to behave, but I couldn't help overhearing classmates talking about sexual things from time to time. I had so many questions to ask, so many worries. I tried reading about it, but if my mother found any books or any pamphlets in the house, she would throw them in the garbage, even if they were library books and I had to pay for them. She declared they shouldn't be in a school library anyway, especially a parochial school.

"Once, I tried hiding a book from her. That was when I discovered my mother went through my room daily, searching everywhere for lascivious material, even under the mattress," I said.

"It sounds like you live in a prison, not a home," Jade said.

"I've felt that way, yes," I admitted.

"My room is my world. Neither of my parents would dare to invade it," she said. "We're people, too, despite our ages. It's stupid to think that just because we're under eighteen, we're some kind of lesser creature."

"Right," Misty said nodding.

"It bothered me along with so many other things. I was more emotional than ever. Sometimes, I would just lay in bed and cry. I had no specific reason for it. Tears would suddenly build and flow and I would shudder and sob. If my mother heard as she passed by my room, she ignored it. Intimate talk not only embarrassed her;

it disgusted her. I felt so lost and confused. It made everything harder."

"What about your father?" Star asked. "After all, he told you that you were his special little girl, right?"

"My father was very busy at the time. He had moved to another brokerage house and was establishing himself and the clients he had brought over with him.

"Everything about our lives was routine then. One day seemed no different from the next, even the weekends blended into the week. All my premature development did was make me feel lonelier than ever. I truly did think of myself as being freakish and I tried to stop thinking about it. I tried to do what my mother wanted, but I was like a rubber band being stretched and stretched until I was about to snap."

"Didn't you have any friends to talk with?" Misty asked.

"I was terrified of personal talk and the other girls knew it. Most of the time, they teased me. Every time one of them brought up a topic related to sex or boys, I felt my ears shut and my body tighten. I usually would find an excuse to leave. I guess by my own behavior I added to the image of being freakish and weird. No one really wanted me as a friend.

"Don't think I didn't feel terrible about it. Other girls went to each other's homes. There were parties, none of which I was invited to. I rarely went to the movies. I felt like I was standing on the other side of a wall, a glass wall, looking in at the rest of the world.

"One night I sat in my tub and sobbed so hard I created waves. Mother was downstairs doing needlepoint. I heard my bedroom door open and close and moments later, there was Daddy looking in at me. He smiled.

" 'What's all this? Why are you crying, Cathy?' he asked.

"I shook my head. I couldn't explain it to myself. How could I explain it to him or anyone else for that matter?

"He saw the redness around my bosom and under my arms and looked concerned.

" 'What's this?' he asked. 'What is it, a rash?' He approached the tub and knelt down to look closer.

" 'No,' I told him. 'It's from the sports bras Mother makes me wear.'

" 'This isn't good,' he said with concern. 'My poor special little girl.'

"He rose and went to the bathroom cabinet and then he returned with some cold cream. First, he rubbed around my bosom, and under my arms with a towel, drying the skin. Then he told me to just sit back and relax as he dabbed the cold cream on and gently spread it over my chest.

" 'Good,' he whispered. 'That's good. It feels better, doesn't it?' he asked as he moved those long, spidery fingers around, under and over my bosom.

"It did feel better. When I opened my eyes, he was looking down at me with such a bright hot look in his eyes, I was both frightened and confused for a moment. Then he spoke softly again and promised to talk to my mother about the terrible thing the sports bras were doing.

"He leaned over and kissed me softly on the forehead. In my house, kisses were as rare as exotic birds.

Every one I received, I cherished in my heart, I hoarded like a jewel in my treasure chest of affection. It had a long way to go to be filled.

"Anyway, if my father did speak to my mother about the problem with the sports bras, she never acknowledged it. She didn't ask or come to look. I continued to complain and on each occasion she told me what she always told me. It wasn't the proper time for me to wear anything else. If I did, it would just emphasize my awkward development and draw looks and comments that would upset and embarrass me.

"Finally, I rebelled and refused to wear the tight exercise bra. When she saw I was going to attend school with only a blouse covering my bosom, she relented and bought me a regular bra, but I seemed to outgrow them as fast as she bought them and that displeased her.

"Once, she even considered bringing me to a doctor and you already know how desperate she would have to be before she would think about doing it.

" 'Maybe there is something terribly wrong with your hormones,' she considered. That frightened me again. She made it sound like I might grow so big, I'd be in a circus. I tried to find something in the library that would explain it or tell me how to slow it down.

"In the seventh grade, we had a unit on sex education, but it was so vague and general, I didn't feel I had learned anything significant about myself. Sister Anne wouldn't permit specific questions or any question that she termed out of line. I learned more just listening to the girls talk in the locker room and bathroom, but never enough to put myself at ease.

"The only time I felt like I wasn't a freak was when

Daddy came in to see me. He told me he wanted to check to be sure the rash hadn't returned and he thought it was best to dab on the cream. He always seemed to see some redness, even if I didn't.

"Once, after I finished my bath, he asked me to lay face down on the bed and he rubbed in body oil he said would make my skin softer. He put it everywhere. When I giggled because he tickled, he told me to hold my breath instead. He didn't want my mother hearing and learning our little secret."

I stopped and took a breath. I had been talking quickly because I felt if I took too long, I would stop and not be able to start again.

Just at that moment, we heard a tray of glasses tinkling and moments later, Emma, Doctor Marlowe's sister, appeared in the office doorway, carrying her usual tray of glasses, pitcher of lemonade and some cookies. Today she wore a pretty pearl white blouse with a lace collar and an ankle-length dark blue skirt. She had some make-up on, too, and her hair was brushed and neatly pinned.

"Good morning, everyone," she said. "Sorry I wasn't here to greet you, but I had a nasty time in the dentist's office. I'm going to have to have a root canal, I'm afraid," she said with a sad face. Then, she quickly smiled. "But it's not the end of the world."

The girls all stared up at her and I knew what they were thinking. Emma had a bosom nearly twice as big as mine. I knew all the jokes like 'They're so big they arrive in a room ten minutes before her.' I had heard boys say these things about me. Was this what I would look like someday?

She put the tray on the table and stepped back.

"Do you need anything else, Doctor Marlowe?" she asked her sister.

"No, thank you, Emma."

"Well, everyone looks cheery this morning, despite the nasty weather. I'll see about the lunch," she added, suddenly made nervous by our silence. She glanced at Doctor Marlowe and then hurried away.

"Dig in, girls," Doctor Marlowe said, rising. "I just want to make one phone call during our break."

She smiled at me, rose and went to her desk. Star poured herself a glass of lemonade and Misty took a cookie. Then she offered me one. I shook my head.

"I'll just have some lemonade," I said.

"Why is your mother so uptight?" Star asked. I'm sure even she was afraid to ask me any more questions about my father.

"Something must have happened in her childhood," Jade ventured. "Maybe . . . she was raped when she was a little girl," she suggested with big, teacup saucer eyes. "Was she raped?"

"I don't know," I said. "If she was, she would never tell me. She never has told me anything about the baby she lost. I already explained how she feels about even making a reference to things like that."

"She needs a therapist more than you do, or any of us do," Jade said.

"She had her visit with Doctor Marlowe, just like your parents, but she doesn't believe in therapy. She almost didn't bring me here today."

"Right, don't air your dirty laundry or something," Star said.

I smiled and nodded.

"Cat, you need some friends, and some help."

"Maybe we can be her friends," Misty suggested.

"Us? We're here because we're screwed up, too, aren't we? That's the blind leading the blind," Star said. "She needs normal friends."

"I'm normal," Jade said indignantly. "Just as normal as most anyone out there. Maybe even more normal."

Star lifted her eyebrows.

"We heard your story; don't try to convince us you're more normal." Before Jade could respond, she added, "And you heard ours. Let's not pretend we don't have problems or excess baggage, okay?"

"We can still be her friends," Jade insisted.

"Maybe she doesn't want us to be her friends." She put her hands on her hips. "You just keep sticking your rich nose into everyone's life all the time, I bet."

"You think you know all about me just because of these sessions? You don't know all about me. You don't know enough to pass judgment on me or anyone. You're the one who's being arrogant."

"Right. You're always right," Star quipped. She turned to me. "Well, you heard us talk about our problems. Do you want anyone here to be your friend?"

"Yes," I admitted. "I would like that."

Jade bit into a cookie and looked gleefully happy. Star rolled her eyes.

"Maybe you're just a lost cause. Maybe we all are. What did you call us, Misty, Orphans With Parents?" Star asked her.

"That's right."

"Okay," Star said. "I nominate Jade here to be president of the OWP."

"I second it," Misty said laughing.

"Who says I want to be president?" Jade quipped.

"You want to be the standout everywhere you go. It doesn't take a genius to see that."

Jade stared at her for a moment and then nodded.

"Okay, I accept. I'm the president," she said.

"Wait, we have to vote. All in favor raise your hand." We all did.

"Done," Star said. "We're the OWP's and Jade is the president."

Everyone laughed as Doctor Marlowe returned. She gazed down at us and smiled.

"Did I miss something important?" she asked.

"Just an election," Star said.

Doctor Marlowe's look of confusion made us all laugh again.

I can do this, I kept thinking. I drank some more lemonade. I can do it.

5

"When I was in the eighth grade, something terrible happened to me," I continued after everyone had had her lemonade and sat back again. I glanced at Doctor Marlowe. She hadn't given me or anyone else here any instructions about what to tell and what not to tell. She looked like she wasn't sure herself what we might say and was just as interested in finding out.

"I suppose now when I look back, it wasn't as horrible as I had thought, but at the time . . . It took a while before I could talk about this after it had happened," I continued. "I kept it a secret from my parents, and actually, I still haven't told my mother about it. I knew she would find a way somehow to blame me, and I was afraid that if I told my father, he might tell her even accidentally, so I swallowed it down like bitter medicine and kept it inside even though it came up like rotten eggs almost every night, leaving me in a cold sweat and bringing me to tears of ice."

No one spoke. They hardly breathed. It was so quiet for a moment, we could hear the sound of leaf-blowers blocks away as gardeners worked behind the high walls of expensive homes. The dull, monotonous sound of their engines seemed to be the proper sound track behind a gray, heavily overcast day.

"What was it already?" Misty blurted. I saw Jade kick her and she sat back, biting down on her lip.

"Whenever I was lucky enough to have someone at school try to be friends with me, my mother usually found a way to stop it. She had watched some guest on a talk show discussing the problems with young people in today's society and she agreed with the conclusion that it was all happening because young people were a bigger influence on each other than their parents.

" 'Peer pressure is stronger than family,' she declared as if it was a major new discovery. It was practically the only time I heard her lead a discussion at dinner. She was so excited about the conclusion, she couldn't stop talking about it to my father, who looked bored, but politely listened and as usual, agreed.

"After that, whenever I mentioned another girl at school, my mother put me through a cross-examination that probably was more severe than a cross-examination during the Spanish Inquisition." I laughed. "I remember watching those court shows on television sometimes and imagining my mother in the courtroom, questioning the defendants, drilling them with biting questions as she fixed her eyes on their faces, catching every tiny revealing movement in their lips or in the way they shifted their gazes.

"You don't lie to my mother. That's one thing you don't do," I said almost proudly.

"You've got to be able to lie to your parents sometimes," Jade said.

Misty nodded vigorously. "Jade's right. It's better for them and better for you. What they don't know, won't hurt them."

"It was just the opposite with my mother," Star said. "She wouldn't know the truth if she tripped over it. She was more comfortable with lies."

"Did you lie about something or just not tell the whole truth?" Misty asked me. She smiled. "That's the way I get around things sometimes."

"I guess I did a combination of both," I said. "But not in the beginning. I was too nervous and afraid to do that. As I said, all I had to do was mention a girl's name and my mother would stop whatever she was doing and turn on me.

" 'Where were you with her? What did she say exactly? What did she mean by that? Who are her parents? Where does she live? What does she look like?'

"She would ask her questions in shotgun fashion, shaking her head and spitting out another before I had a chance to answer the one before. The more I didn't know about the girl, the worse it was. Usually, she would end by forbidding me to talk to her again and I'd have to remember to never mention that girl's name."

Jade spun angrily on Doctor Marlowe.

"How can you let her continue to live with such a monster? She hits her. She won't let her make friends.

She treats her like she's something dirty. Why don't you tell the authorities?"

Doctor Marlowe closed her eyes softly and opened them with a gentle smile.

"Cathy has a great deal more to say and you should hear it all before you come to any conclusions, Jade. You wouldn't have liked it any other way, would you?"

Jade turned back to me, still fuming, her arms wrapped tightly around herself, her eyes bright with anger.

"Your mother's a Nazi," she muttered.

I didn't laugh or reply. I waited for a surge of nausea to pass and then I took a breath and continued.

"There was this girl, Kelly Sullivan, whose father works for the church in some administrative capacity. I think he manages properties or something. Her mother is in a wheelchair. She has multiple sclerosis. They live in a nice, ranch-style house only about ten minutes by car from us.

"Kelly has beautiful green eyes and apricot red hair. She's a lot smaller than me, slimmer, I should say, but most girls who were my age in the eighth grade were. She hated her freckles. There were patches of them on each check and even on the bottom of her chin, but she had a pretty face. She thought her freckles made her look like a freak and of course, I had my problem. Her parents were like my mother in that they didn't want Kelly to wear any makeup, not even lipstick. I actually thought she and I had a lot in common and for a while, I had hopes that she would be a real best friend. We often talked in the cafeteria and we shared three classes. She had other friends, but she didn't seem to me to be that popular. She was shy in school and when she met my mother, she was so sweet and polite, my mother looked at her with such approval and pleasure, I was actually jealous.

"I mean, Kelly had almost no figure yet, which my mother thought was good and normal, and Kelly was full of please's and thank you's, just the recipe for the kind of little girl my mother wanted. I had been talking about her enough for my mother to finally consent to my bringing her home with me one afternoon. I was afraid to, afraid that once Kelly met my mother and had my mother grill her with questions, she would never want to talk to me again, but I liked Kelly and wanted her for a friend and knew if I didn't have Mother's approval, I couldn't. I was very nervous about it.

"However, as I said, to my surprise Mother liked her even more than I had hoped she would. She seemed pleased that Kelly's mother was an invalid and she was especially pleased that her father was working for the church.

"Even so, my mother was very cautious and hesitant about my going to Kelly's house to study for tests together. The first time, she permitted me to go for only two hours and after exactly two hours, she was in the driveway waiting. I knew as soon as I got into the car, she would question me about every moment I spent with Kelly.

"We did study some, but we also listened to music and talked to other girls and some boys on the phone. Kelly's mother was a sweet pleasant woman and I envied Kelly for the trusting and loving relationship they had. I almost wished my mother was in a wheelchair. Maybe if she was seriously ill, she would be a more loving mother, I thought, and then I hated myself for wishing such a terrible thing."

Jade grunted and then agreed, "Maybe she wouldn't be so mean if she had to depend on you."

"Yeah," Star said. I didn't want to discuss such a thing. I still felt guilty for even thinking it.

"Kelly's father was very nice, too, and I could see how much he loved and cherished Kelly's mother," I continued instead.

"Anyway, I guess because I had gone to Kelly's house a few times and nothing horrible had happened, my mother was a little less concerned when I asked if I could go to dinner there one Friday night."

I paused and then added for Misty's benefit, "It wasn't the whole truth. I mean, we were going to eat, but it wasn't really a dinner. We were going to have pizza and Kelly had invited two other girls and some boys."

"So it was a party," Misty said.

"I guess. I had never been to a party at someone's house, so I didn't know what to call it. Kelly didn't tell me all the details right away. In fact, I didn't even know the boys were coming until that afternoon in school. It made my heart race with fear. I was terrified that my mother would find out somehow. Maybe when she drove me there, the boys would just be arriving or maybe she would take one look at my face and that lie detector in her head would ring. I tried to avoid her as soon as I got home, but she called me downstairs to recite a list of rules for my behavior.

"I sat with my hands folded in my lap as she stood before me in the living room. My father wasn't home from work yet. Sometimes, he stopped at a tavern with some of his stockbroker associates and celebrated or mourned the day's results in the market.

" 'We don't say grace before we eat every night,' my mother began, 'but we should. It's your father's fault, not mine. Anyway, don't look stupid about it and don't let them know we don't. It's no one's business. Bow your head and make sure you pronounce your amen loud and clear, understand?' she asked me.

" 'Yes, Mother,' I said eying the door and trying not to look guilty of anything.

" 'Don't stare at her mother in the wheelchair.'

" 'I wouldn't do that, Mother.'

" 'We don't adhere to proper dinner etiquette either, not that I permit you to be sloppy or impolite at the table. It's just that your father never cared for formal dining. I have everything set up in the dining room,' she told me. 'Now get up and follow me.'

"I did and I was surprised at the lengths she had gone to in order to give me instructions. She had a book of dining etiquette out and open. She had taken out every piece of silverware we owned, and our finest china with her nicest linen dinner napkins.

" 'Sit,' she ordered, pointing at my place. Then she picked up the book and held it like a Bible in her open palms. She even sounded like some kind of Sunday School teacher.

" 'You should know that the silverware is placed in the order of its use, with the implements to be used first farthest from the plate. The salad fork is placed next to the left of the plate, then the meat fork, which they might not have out, being this is Friday night, and then the fish fork which will be used first. Just to the right of the plate is the salad knife, next is the meat knife, which again, might not be there, and on the outside is the fish knife. Outside the knives are the soup spoon and, if they have it, the fruit spoon. Dessert forks and spoons should be brought in on the dessert plate, but they might have it out already. I don't know how formal they are, of course. You know what the butter plate is and how it's there for your bread. Remember not to put your elbows on the table or slurp your soup or talk with food in your mouth. Any questions?'

" 'No, Mother,' I said. I was dying inside, knowing that all we actually were going to do was open a few boxes of pizza and probably slap the pieces on paper plates, and open bottles of soda. Now I was even more terrified of her learning the truth. She might accuse me of making a big fool out of her.

"My teeth were practically chattering when it was time for her to take me over to Kelly's house. I was afraid she might go in with me, but my mother, fortunately, is shy herself, and just let me get out of the car.

" 'Call me when it's time to come home and remember, don't overstay your welcome, Cathy. Oh, wipe your mouth after every bite and always say please and thank you when you're passed anything at the table. Don't speak unless you're asked a question,' she warned.

" 'Okay,' I muttered with my head down and hurried to the front door, praying no one else would arrive before my mother pulled away. No one did because they were already in the house. I didn't know Kelly's parents weren't home. Her father had taken her mother out to dinner.

"In fact, when Kelly opened the door for me, the music was so loud, I was afraid it might spill out and reach my mother's car even as she drove away.

"I was a little shocked. It was as if Kelly had become a different person. She was wearing a blouse tied at her waist instead of buttoned so some uncovered waist showed, and a pair of jeans with no shoes or socks. Here I was dressed in my best outfit.

" 'She's here!' Kelly screamed and the others came out of her room.

"I guess I was standing there with my mouth fallen open. Everyone laughed at me and how formally I was dressed. Everyone else was in jeans and T-shirts. I didn't know the boys, of course, and they were quickly introduced. I was too nervous to pay much attention to their full names. Michael was a tall, dark boy with light brown hair and brown eyes, Tony was a shorter boy, stout, with very light brown hair and very nice blue eyes, and Frankie was a rather heavy boy with black hair and dark eyes. Talia Morris was there and so was Jill Brewster, girls I knew from school, but not very well. I found out that Tony was Jill's older brother and he had brought his friends. Tony, Frankie and Michael attended public school.

"My second shock came when I discovered that the cups they held in their hands were not filled with just Coke. Tony had brought a bottle of rum. A cup was thrust at me immediately, and I held it like I would hold a loaded pistol when I was told what was in it.

" 'I can't drink this,' I told them. 'My mother will smell it on me immediately.'

" 'Don't worry about that. You chew some gum or gargle with mouthwash. We're very experienced with all this,' Tony assured me. 'We even drink it at school sometimes,' he added, laughing. 'Come on, join the party.' He practically forced me to sip the drink. I didn't taste the rum, but I know it was in there because it wasn't too long before I felt myself grow light-headed and a little dizzy.

"I guess I was fascinated by it all. The boys had so many outrageous stories to tell about life at their school. Compared to ours, it sounded exciting to be there every day. I sat back on Kelly's bed and listened and watched as they played music, smoked, drank some more rum and Coke, always filling my cup as well. We devoured the pizza when it was delivered. I laughed a lot and for a while, I felt so happy and good. I especially enjoyed the girls' conversation when they made fun of the sisters and our life in the parochial school. For me this was like being in another country. I was shocked by some of the things said, of course, but I tried not to show it.

"I didn't want to smoke, but they were all doing it and it seemed impossible not to do something everyone else was doing. Vaguely, I thought, my mother was right about peer pressure. It is the strongest thing, but I shook that idea out of my head or to be more honest, the rum drowned it.

"Something happened in that confused brain of mine. Suddenly, everyone looked so silly to me. I start-ed to laugh at the way Michael rolled his eyes after sipping his drink and puffing his cigarette, taking such care to look cool and sophisticated about it. He raised his eyebrows into question marks and looked at me, and then I laughed again and it felt like a dam had broken. I couldn't stop giggling. That struck them funny and they laughed too, which only made me laugh harder until tears began to stream down my face.

"Frankie suddenly sat beside me and slipped his arm around my shoulders.

" 'I better hold her before she breaks apart. She's jiggling too much!' he cried and they all roared. It seemed no one could stop the roller coaster. He held me tighter and tighter and soon I could see the faces of the other two boys change a little. They stopped laughing and suddenly looked intensely interested in me. Kelly, Talia, and Jill drew closer to each other and watched, whispering. What were they all looking at? I wondered, and then gazed down and saw that Frankie had his hand in my blouse. One of the buttons of my blouse had come undone and he was undoing another and another.

"For a moment even I was confused about it. Then his fingers lifted the underside of my bra and exposed my breast.

" 'Let's see if everything's all right,' he declared.

" 'Stop!' I screamed and pulled away, but when I rose, I stumbled into Tony's arms, only instead of catching me, he put his hands on my bosom and held me up that way, his left hand smack over my naked breast.

" 'It's all right. Yeah,' he declared. Everyone was laughing, even the girls.

" 'My turn!' Michael said coming up behind me. 'There's enough for all of us.'

"He reached over and cupped my breasts, lifting my bra off the left side, too, and pulled me back against him. I lost my footing and slid down his body to the floor. Everyone kept laughing, but I started crying and that finally ended it.

"The girls took me to the bathroom where I threw up. They helped me clean up and kept assuring me it was all right and the boys would behave now. I had such a splitting headache, but all I could think was my mother would find out everything. I went into a crying jag.

"The boys left shortly afterward, maybe because they were afraid of getting in trouble, and things quieted down. Kelly's parents came home. Her father looked a little suspicious when he saw me sitting in practically a coma on the bed, but he didn't ask any questions, even though I imagined I looked very pale. The girls assured me they couldn't smell any rum on me. I went outside with Kelly and Talia and took deep breaths of air until I felt well enough to chance calling my mother.

" 'I hope you don't say anything about this,' Kelly warned me. 'You'll get me in a lot of trouble and you'll only get yourself in trouble, too.'

" 'You should have told me what was going to happen,' I scolded.

" 'Don't be a prude,' Talia said. 'You had a good time, didn't you?'

"I remember looking at her as if she was crazy. Boys had molested me. I had thrown up. I had a good time?

" 'No,' I said sullenly.

"I was so frightened when my mother came, I don't know how I walked out and got into the car.

" 'How was the dinner?' she asked immediately.

" 'Very nice,' I said.

" 'Did they serve fish?'

" 'No,' I said. At least that wasn't a lie.

" 'And did you behave? Did you follow all the rules of etiquette? Oh, did they start with grace?' she asked quickly before I could answer her other questions.

"I thought for a moment and said, 'Yes. It all happened the way you told me it might.'

"It was dark in the car so she wasn't able to search my eyes and see the deception. I bit down on my lip and held my breath in anticipation.

"However, she liked hearing she was right to teach me all about dinner etiquette and such and for the remainder of the ride home, she congratulated herself on being wise enough to prepare me well.

" 'Your father wouldn't know the first thing about it,' she told me, 'despite his sophistication in business. When he saw all I had done for you, he laughed and thought it was ridiculous. Now he'll see,' she said nodding. 'Now we'll see how smug he is.'

"When we arrived home, I was able to go right upstairs, claiming I was tired. She didn't question it. She was too eager to tell my father how well she had prepared me for the dinner. I crawled into bed as quickly as I could. When I thought about what had happened, I cried. How embarrassing it was and how terrible it was that the other girls didn't come to my defense. It was almost as if I had been invited there just to be abused. When would I ever have a real friend, someone who cared about me and my feelings?

"It made me feel so dirty to recall their hands over

me. I think that was a major reason why my stomach turned over and I got so sick, that and the rum. How much had I drunk? Did the girls know what the boys were doing to me and let them?"

"I wish we knew you then," Star piped up. "I'd pay them a visit for you."

"Very immature behavior," Jade commented.

"It was cruel," Misty agreed.

"The hardest thing about having something unpleasant happen to you is having no one to tell at the time," I told them. "It festers like a sore, an infection; it buzzes around in your head and your heart. I tossed and turned and fretted through nightmares for nights after that and I couldn't face the other girls at school. I knew they were talking about me, spreading stories, exaggerating, claiming I had gotten drunk and exposed myself in front of the boys and embarrassed them. Kelly avoided me and I felt even worse because of the way some of the other girls were now looking at me."

"Why would they lie about her like that?" Misty asked Jade.

"To protect themselves in case she did tell someone the truth. Right?" Jade asked Star.

"Sounds like it. I would have pulled out their tongues at that point," Star said.

"It would only make them look right," Jade asserted.

"Maybe because of the way things were at school, my nightmares continued. I had no appetite at dinner, but I had to force myself to eat so my mother wouldn't ask any questions. The hardest thing was she kept asking me about Kelly's parents, the house, things they said, and I had to make up as much as I could. I got

79

away with it because I told my mother I had followed her directions and not asked too many questions. I kept thinking, Soon, soon she's going to realize I'm lying and the whole horrible thing will come out.

"That gave me even more nightmares. Many nights I would find myself awake, practically sitting up, listening to the scream die in my throat. In dreams I felt spiders crawling over me, dozens and dozens of them. They covered my breasts and reached as high as my chin.

"When I was a little girl and I had bad dreams, my mother would sometimes come to see me, but she never held me or kissed me. Instead, she tried to teach me how to block out unpleasantness. She told me to count until I was so tired, I would fall asleep again. Reluctantly, because I begged her, she would leave a light on in the bathroom.

"One night nearly two weeks after the disastrous party at Kelly's and all the questions and lying, I heard my door open and close and my father stood in the darkness at my bedside.

" 'What's wrong?' he asked. 'I thought I heard you cry out when I came up from getting myself a glass of milk.'

"He did that if he ever had any trouble sleeping. He once told me that sometimes numbers from the stock market keep playing as if he had a ticker tape machine in his head as soon as he closed his eyes.

"I just turned my head into the pillow until I felt his hand on my shoulder and felt him sit on my bed.

" 'Something wrong with my special girl?' he asked. I couldn't help myself. I started to cry again. He stroked my hair and waited.

" 'What is it?' he asked. 'You can tell me. Did someone do something or say something that upset you?'

" 'Yes,' I admitted in a small voice.

" 'Yes what?' he demanded. 'It's better you tell me,' he added.

"I swallowed down my tears and quietly told him what had happened at Kelly's house. He listened without speaking, but I could feel his eyes fixed firmly on me, even in the dark.

" 'Is it my fault?' I wanted to know. 'Am I bad?'

" 'No, no,' he said, and then he leaned over and put his lips to my ear and added, 'There's good touching and bad. You shouldn't be afraid of the good or be ashamed of it.

" 'Boys who grope girls are bad. It doesn't make you feel good inside, right?'

" 'No,' I agreed. He was definitely right about that, and if he was right about that, why wouldn't he be right about the rest of it?

" 'Good touching is gentle, soft,' he said and as he spoke, he showed me.

" 'Close your eyes,' he said. 'That's it. You shouldn't be afraid to sleep,' he whispered. His hands were under my nightgown and he moved his fingers softly, gently over me as he chanted, 'Be still, be happy. See, this is good touching. It's like petting a dog or a cat,' he said, 'and you know how that pleases them. See, it's pleasing you. You'll sleep now.'

"His touching didn't relax me. It felt like a tense wire was coiling tighter and tighter inside my stomach. His hands were soft, gentle, but they were moving everywhere, and it made me even more nervous than I already had been.

" 'Easy,' he said when I tried to squirm away. 'You've got to relax your body and not be afraid of good feelings.'

"I kept myself as still as I could.

" 'That's it,' he said. 'That's better. See?'

"My body felt tense. I tried to keep my eyes closed and go to sleep, but it was hard to relax with him still touching me. Finally, he stopped and stood up.

" 'Good night,' he whispered. 'We'll keep it all secret,' he promised. 'All that's happened will be part of our big special secret. Don't worry. Your mother doesn't have to know. It would only upset her anyway and we don't want to do that, do we? Cathy?'

"He needed to hear my answer. My voice cracked, but I managed.

" 'No,' I said. My heartbeat was so quick, I couldn't catch my breath.

"Moments later, he was gone and I fell into a pool of confusion, my body in a turmoil and yet, I was happy I was still able to be my daddy's special girl, happy I wasn't a bad girl in his eyes."

I paused. The three were so still, their eyes unmoving, their lips frozen.

"Well," Doctor Marlowe said after a moment, "why don't we take another break and I'll see about lunch."

No one moved; no one spoke.

"Anyone need to go to the bathroom or anything?"

"I do," Misty said rising. She looked at me. "Unless you have to go first."

"No, I'm fine," I said.

CAT

The rain had started. The wind blew drops against the window and they zigzagged their way down like crooked tears. When I looked back at Jade, she was staring at the floor. Star was gazing out the window. She looked so deep in thought it made my heart skip a beat. Their silence was louder than the thunder rolling in from the storm.

Despite feeling somewhat drained, I still thought I could do this. Doctor Marlowe had brought me to this stage in my therapy, holding my hand, consoling me and building my confidence until I thought it would be all right, but as I looked at the others, I suddenly wondered, can they do it? What nightmares and fears had I stirred in their vaults of horrid memories?

The four of us were chained together by our pain now, and the trembling one felt reached through the hearts of the next and the next and the next until we all trembled together. Was it good to share or was it cruel?

Every question raised another.

Answers taunted us with promises just like beautiful fish beneath the water, and when we reached too quickly or too deeply, they were gone in a flash, leaving us waiting, searching, hoping for another opportunity.

How could we not be afraid they would never come back, even to taunt us?

6

"**I** hate days like this," Jade said after a long moment of silence. "I know it hardly rains here compared to most other places, and I guess I'm spoiled, but I can't stand this dreary weather."

"I don't mind it so much," Misty said. "Unless it's day after day."

"Granny hates it because it stirs up her aches and pains," Star said.

"Too many days look gray and gloomy to me without the clouds and rain," Jade admitted.

"It's not that bad," Misty insisted. Jade didn't like to be contradicted.

"I suppose if you live like a child in a fantasy world, it doesn't matter," she said, fixing her gaze on Misty.

"I don't live in a fantasy world and I don't live like a child."

"We all do," I said and they turned to me. "I mean, if

you aren't happy with things, you daydream a lot, don't you? I do," I confessed. "And you've all described doing it in one way or another, too."

"Cat's right," Star said, nodding. She glanced at Jade. "There's no point lying to each other just because everyone else lies to us."

"I spend a lot of time in my room, alone, just . . . dreaming," I told them, "a lot of time. That's what made my parents want me to see Doctor Marlowe in the first place. I hated stepping out the front door, hated going to school, just hated leaving the house at all. I missed a lot of school, claiming headaches and stomach cramps or just being too tired. It got so bad the nuns were talking to my mother about getting me a home tutor, and you know how much she would hate having a stranger in our home every day."

"Do you have a nice house?" Misty asked.

"It's okay, but it's nothing like this. We've got a good size backyard. The property's walled-in with oleander bushes growing up the walls to give us lots of privacy. My mother's always planting something that will close it in more. Mostly it's just grass and a couple of grapefruit and lemon trees. My father used to talk about building a pool. My mother would ask, 'What for?' and he would look at her as if he was giving it lots of thought and then say, 'To swim in.'

" 'It's too much work,' my mother muttered, 'and with your schedule, who's going to do it?'

"He said he would hire someone just like everyone else he knew who had a pool, but the discussion usually ended with that and nothing was ever done.

"I used to think if we had a pool, I could invite some

girls over, but then I thought, what kind of bathing suit would my mother approve? Certainly not a bikini, and who would I invite anyway and suppose I found some girls who would come and they wore bikinis. Mother would ask them to leave."

"Well, if you invited friends over now, you could hang out in your bedroom, right?" Misty asked, and I wondered if she would ever want to visit.

"I suppose. You all would probably think my room was too plain. I don't have any posters or pictures up. It's probably not as big as yours or Jade's, but at least it has two big windows that face east so I get the morning sunlight. I have a pinkish gray rug and a double bed with a mahogany headboard and two posts at the foot of the bed. Beside the mirror and dresser, I have my desk, another dresser and bookshelves built into the wall. I don't have a television set or a phone in the room. My mother would never permit either. She says they're both bad influences on young people."

"It sounds like you're trapped in a cage," Jade muttered.

"Oh, our house isn't that small. We have a good size living room with a fireplace and large panel windows that face the west so there's lots of afternoon sunshine. Mother hung thick drapes to block it out when she wants to. The kitchen is big. My mother likes to cook and bake. I wouldn't call her a gourmet cook like you have, Jade, but she's good at making traditional meals and pies. That was one thing my father always complimented, her food. He was a meat and potatoes man."

"So he married her for her cooking and money, is that it?" Jade asked dryly.

"Didn't they fall in love first?" Misty followed quickly.

"I never actually came out and asked either of them when or how they fell in love. I guess I never felt they had and the little I did learn about their past convinced me I was right. They didn't date and have a romance like your parents or Jade's. My mother's father actually met my father first. He started to invest with him. He either mentioned my mother or introduced him to her one day and that was how they got to know each other.

"My mother didn't have a job and never went to college. When I asked her why not once, she told me there wasn't anything she wanted to be. She was an okay student, but not very ambitious, I guess. I think it upset my grandfather. From the little my mother has told me, I don't think they had a good relationship because he was so critical of her, telling her she would be a spinster and amount to nothing if she remained at home, just helping her mother with the housework and the meals.

"Sometimes, I got the feeling she got married to stop my grandfather's criticism. It wasn't exactly an arranged marriage, but my grandfather seems to have had a lot to do with it. She keeps her wedding album practically hidden away on a shelf in the living room. I used to look at it occasionally. She doesn't look bright and happy in her wedding pictures; it's more like she's going through the motions, doing something that has to be done, but something without passion and excitement. It doesn't look like a special day for her.

"It would have to be something very special for me," I said. "I mean, you should just glow in your wedding pictures, don't you think? The photographer shouldn't even need flashbulbs because your face is so lit up, right? I'd love to be fulfilled and loved by someone who made me so happy I glowed."

Misty laughed. Jade smiled and shook her head, and Star raised her eyebrows and nodded.

"No," I continued considering their questions more, "I don't think my parents ever felt that way about each other or had time for love, not the way you talked about your own parents and their romances," I told them. "When I asked my mother where they went on their honeymoon, she told me they just went straight home.

" 'There was plenty to do to set it up,' she said, 'and there was no point in wasting money on some over-priced vacation where they charge you twice the price for everything you can get at home.' "

"If she thinks like that, she'll never go anywhere," Jade said.

"She doesn't. Don't you remember what Cat told us about taking trips?" Star pointed out.

"Have you lived in the same house all your life?" Misty asked.

"Yes. My mother is not one who likes change, even small changes like wallpaper or rugs, much less a move to another house. Lots of times now, I wish we would move. The house seems stained with bad memories for me, and as long as we're there, I can't help but imagine my father is still there."

"Did you ever ask her why they adopted you?" Jade asked. "I know you told us that you didn't think they had sex much, if at all after your mother lost the baby, but it still doesn't explain why they would adopt you, or anyone for that matter."

"No. Like I told you, my adoption was something I discovered just recently, after . . . after other stuff happened. It's hard for my mother to talk about it right now."

"Hard for her to talk about it?" Jade cried with indignation. "They always act like they're the ones who are suffering, like we can endure the pain because we're young. Nothing scars us; nothing really hurts us. We'll outgrow it, even betrayals and broken promises. Hard for her? Your mother hasn't got a right to be more upset than you. Don't let her get away with it," she advised. "Ask her anything you want and insist on an answer. You deserve it."

"Yeah, if she refuses to tell you what you want, threaten to wear lipstick and eye shadow," Star suggested.

Misty laughed and I smiled, and we were all laughing when Doctor Marlowe returned. She looked very pleased.

"Well, I hope you all are hungry. As usual, Emma has gone overboard with lunch."

They all looked at me to see what I wanted and what I would say.

"I guess I am hungry," I said.

Anyway, I thought, I'll need my strength if I'm to go on with my story.

Lunch was truly a break for us. I think they needed it as much as I did. We talked about everything but our home life and our parents and the things that had brought us here in the first place. However, I wasn't anywhere as up-to-date as any of them when it came to movies and music.

"I don't know how you listen to that hip-hop," Jade told Star. "It's so monotonous."

"It is not. You haven't given it a chance. That's why you say that. Who do you like?"

"I like Barry Manilow," Misty admitted. "I do," she insisted, "and I've even been to three of his concerts."

"What about you, Cat?" Jade asked me.

"I guess I like everything or whatever I get to hear, that is. My mother hates me listening to any music too long. She thinks it hurts my schoolwork."

"Get earphones and she won't even know when you're listening," Star suggested.

Doctor Marlowe sat off to the right eating and listening to us without comment. I wondered if the others ever got the feeling we were all under some giant microscope, all being observed and studied. Maybe someday we would get together somewhere else, without therapists or parents, and be free to talk about all this, free to talk without anyone looking at us and studying us.

Or maybe when today ended, we wouldn't see each other ever again. Maybe just the sight of one of us would bring back all the bad memories and they would look for ways to avoid the rest of us, especially me, I thought, especially after I'm finished with my whole story.

I almost didn't feel like going on when lunch was over and we returned to the office. Why not leave it at this? I wondered. I had already gone further than I had expected. Wasn't Doctor Marlowe satisfied?

One look at her face told me no, told me she wanted me to tell them the worst, if not today, than maybe tomorrow, and if I didn't, it would fester and irritate inside me, just as I had told them it would.

They waited for me to begin again. I sucked in my breath and started.

"When I was in the tenth grade, my school sent a letter home with every high school student announcing that the school was sponsoring an annual dance with an all-boys parochial school. The dance was described in detail, when it would start, what food would be served, what we were permitted to wear and not wear, and how well it was going to be chaperoned by the sisters. There was some statement about the importance of healthy, clean social activities and how the dance was an important learning experience for young people. This way we would have something decent to measure the wrong sort of activities against. Parents were actually encouraged to permit their daughters to attend.

"My mother wasn't happy about it, but she was trapped by the fact that the school she admired was promoting it. I recall my father finally offering a firm opinion about something involving me.

" 'The way this is described,' he pointed out after dinner one night, 'it will actually be another learning experience. I should think you'd want her to be in a controlled, healthy environment for something like this, Geraldine.'

"My mother pressed her upper lip over her lower and stared at the school dance announcement as if it were a warrant for my arrest rather than a social affair.

" 'She'll need a new dress,' she said in a discouraging tone of voice.

" 'So? Get her a new dress,' my father said.

"I sat there practically holding my breath. He

winked at me and I felt wonderful. My heart was in a pitter-patter just anticipating the preparations.

" 'The styles these days are so . . . awful. It's hard to get anything decent,' my mother complained.

" 'I'm sure you can find something, somewhere, Geraldine,' he told her, refusing to give in like he usually did. He could see how important this was to me and he was playing my knight in shining armor.

"My mother looked at the announcement again and then at me. I could see she was relenting.

" 'I suppose you'll want to wear lipstick, won't you?' she asked me.

" 'All the girls her age do,' my father said quickly. 'On occasion, there's nothing wrong with it, Geraldine. As long as she doesn't overdo it,' he added.

"I couldn't believe how firmly he was coming to my aid, speaking up for me.

" 'Girls get into trouble so easily these days,' my mother muttered. 'One small thing leads to another and then a bigger thing and before you know it, they're pregnant.'

" 'Oh, I suppose you and I can make sure that something like that doesn't happen to our special little girl,' he said glancing and smiling at me again. When he said, 'special little girl,' my heart skipped a beat and I think I even blushed.

"My mother's eyebrows rose but fortunately, she was staring at him and not me.

" 'Is that so, Howard?' she said. 'You mean you're finally going to take some real responsibility for her?'

" 'I know I've been busy and left a good deal of this to you, Geraldine. I've been remiss on that score, but I'll do my part now that Cathy is getting of age.'

" 'Of age for what?' my mother pounced.

" 'Oh, meeting people, getting out more, learning the ways of the world,' he said calmly.

" 'She's better off not knowing the ways of this world,' my mother insisted.

"They talked about it a little more. My father volunteered to drive me to the school and pick me up after the dance. Finally, she reluctantly agreed even though she added that she thought I was still too young for such a thing."

"And did she agree to permit you to wear lipstick?" Jade asked with a coy smile.

"A little," I said. "Although, she kept the tube in her room after we bought it."

"Where? In the safe?" Jade asked.

"Practically," I said smiling. "The hardest thing was finding a dress she liked. We went to so many department stores, but nothing was right. Finally, she found this small store out in the valley. I think it was more like a costume shop. The hem was low enough to satisfy her. It reached a little below my ankles, and the collar went halfway up my neck. It looked like something from the 1800's. It was too big, too, but she thought that was fine. She found shoes that matched and I had what she considered my new party outfit.

"When I looked at myself in it, I nearly burst into tears. I was sure I would be ridiculed. It had puffy sleeves, lots of lace, and big black buttons on this emerald green heavy cotton material. She had me put it on and model it for my father, who sat there with his eyebrows hoisted.

" 'Looks like she's in a play or something,' he said.

'It's practically a costume. Is that the sort of party dress a girl would wear today?'

" 'It's perfect,' my mother insisted.

" 'I feel stupid in it,' I declared, encouraged by my father's reaction. 'When I walk, I can hear the material swishing around me. It's too loose and I'll choke to death in this collar if I try to eat anything,' I wailed.

" 'It's perfect,' my mother repeated. 'Proper and perfect.'

" 'No boy is going to want to dance with me wearing this,' I complained.

" 'Is that what you're worried about? How many boys will dance with you?' my mother asked.

" 'No, not how many,' I moaned. 'Any.'

"I was nearly in tears about it. I wanted to go to the dance very much. I saw it as my chance to make new friends and maybe to have a social life, too, but I was terrified that wearing that dress would make me look like a buffoon.

" 'Why can't I get something more in style?' I cried.

" 'The styles today are downright pornographic,' my mother said. 'You saw that from the little we viewed in the department stores. And besides, you read the dance announcement and rules. Most of the things on sale in the stores wouldn't be permitted anyway. Be happy you have something decent,' she insisted and left it at that.

"I went upstairs to sulk about it, and later, my father came to my room. He asked me to put on the dress again and I did. Then he stood back, studied it for a moment and stepped forward to unbutton the collar almost down to my cleavage.

" 'That looks better,' he said, 'but don't do it until

94

after you get to the school. You're becoming a very pretty young lady, Cathy, do you know that?' he asked and I felt myself blush all over.

" 'No, I'm not,' I said. 'I'm too big and I don't have any nice features.'

" 'Sure you do,' he said. 'I'm just sorry I haven't had more talks with you about what you should expect now that you are mixing with boys. I'm glad the dance is still a week away. There's a lot I want to tell you, show you, explain to you. Most parents throw their children out to the wolves, especially their daughters, and then wonder why they get themselves into trouble. Your mother thinks the answer is to keep you here under lock and key, but I know the answer is to make you smart and aware so nothing comes as a surprise.

" 'Doesn't that make more sense to you?' he asked me and I nodded because it did sound right.

" 'Tomorrow is a holiday and the market's closed, too. I'll spend some time with you in the afternoon when your mother goes food shopping, okay? I'll help you prepare for the birds and the bees.'

"I had no idea what he meant, but I nodded. He stood there staring at me for a long moment and then he smiled, came forward and kissed me on the cheek.

" 'Don't you smell good,' he said. 'What is that, the bath oil I bought you?'

" 'Yes,' I said. He put his nose against me and inhaled so hard, I thought I might be drawn up his nostrils. Then he planted another small kiss on my neck, patted me on the hip, and left the room.

"You probably wonder why I remember so many details. That was because my father was so confusing to me. Sometimes he acted as if I was invisible and sometimes, he would stop and stare at me so hard, I couldn't help my heart from thumping. This was one of those times."

I paused and gazed down at the floor for a moment. I could feel their eyes on me and then I caught them looking nervously at each other. Doctor Marlowe had templed her fingers beneath her chin and rested her elbows on her knees as she waited, too. Lunch tumbled in my stomach, but I swallowed back any gagging.

For me it was like making a big, wide turn in my story. The worst was yet to come and I knew it, and from the sound of their silence, I knew the girls were aware of it, too. They looked worried for me. They looked like they really cared.

"The next day I hadn't forgotten what my father had said, but I was very occupied with my schoolwork and thinking about the dance. At school all the girls were talking about it. Most of them had been to dances like this before and many knew a number of the boys who would be attending.

"I sat to the side in the cafeteria and listened to the older girls talk about it, trying to learn as much as I could so I wouldn't appear like such a fish out of water when I attended. When I heard some of the girls describe what they were going to wear, my heart sank. Most were going to dress in clothes my mother had vetoed. Everyone but me would be in style.

"I had already been plagued by nightmares in which I arrived at the dance and the whole party stopped as one girl and boy after another looked my way. Even the sisters looked amused at what I wore. Then, they all broke out into hysterical laughter and I ran out of the building into the night, tears streaming down my reddened cheeks.

"I was coming to the conclusion that I shouldn't go to the dance, that it would be worse for me afterward. All my chances to have any sort of normal social life, to make friends, to be invited to anything else, would be washed away the moment I entered that decorated gymnasium, I thought. I decided I just wouldn't go. I was sure my mother would be happy about that decision."

"Damn," Star muttered.

"But," I said, "I didn't have to make that decision."

The girls all widened their eyes and waited.

"After my mother had left the house, my father came to my room. He knocked and entered and under his arm was a big box.

" 'What's that?' I immediately asked.

" 'Part of our special secret,' he told me. 'You better not tell her about this, or I'll be drawn and quartered at sundown the day after your dance,' he warned and put the box on my bed. He stepped back.

"I just stared down at it.

" 'Well, open it and look!' he cried and laughed.

"I approached it slowly and took off the cover. There in the box was a new dress, a real dress, green velvet with a knee-length skirt and spaghetti straps and some beads on the right side. It was the most beautiful dress I had ever seen. He even bought me shoes to match it!

" 'How can I wear this, Daddy?' I asked, astounded. 'Mother won't let me.'

" 'She won't know. You'll put on the dress she made

you buy and after we leave the house, we'll pull over and you'll put on this dress,' he said nodding at the box. 'You won't have a mirror to check yourself out, but I'll be your mirror,' he offered. 'Put it on. Let's see how right I was about your size and such,' he added.

"He stood there with his long arms folded under his chest and waited. My heart was pounding. Changing in front of him was truly doing something forbidden, but I was too excited about my beautiful new dress to care.

"I quickly unbuttoned and removed my blouse, took off my skirt and slipped into the dress. He came behind to zip me up and then he turned me toward the mirror.

" 'Like Cinderella,' he said. 'Look how beautiful you are now.'

"I was actually frightened by my own appearance. The dress fit a bit snugly, especially the bodice, and there was just the suggestion of the beginning of my cleavage. Would the nuns turn me away? Wasn't Daddy afraid of that?

" 'Perfect,' he said instead. 'That's a dress.'

" 'What if Mother hears about this?' I asked him.

" 'It's a green dress, too. Besides, she won't hear about it. Where does she go to be able to hear such things? Well?'

" 'Oh Daddy!' I cried. Tears were filling my eyes. 'Thank you.'

"I gave him a hug and he kissed the top of my head and held on to me for a long moment.

"Then he held me out, at arm's length, looked me over, nodded and smiled.

" 'Now,' he said, 'it's time for your lessons.' "

7

"'**K**eep the dress on,' he ordered. 'Everything should be as close as possible to how it is going to be at the dance.' He thought for a moment. 'We need some music, too. Yes, that's it. We'll turn your room into the school ballroom.'

"He snapped on my radio and found a station.

"'How's that?' he asked about the music.

"I shrugged.

"'I guess it's okay,' I said. I hadn't been to a school dance before, so I had no idea what sort of music would be played, especially at a parochial school dance."

"No hip-hop, I bet," Star said.

"No," I said. "They censor the words in the songs. They wouldn't even play Madonna."

"Some dance," Star muttered.

"'Okay,' Daddy said. 'Let's start at the beginning. You come to the dance and like all the girls, you gather together, talk about everyone's clothes and hairdos. Now,' he added with a wink, 'they'll surely be talking about you. And in a nice way, an enviable way,' he quickly added.

" 'As soon as the boys see you, especially how you look now, you'll be approached by one or more and asked to dance. Be polite. Don't turn anyone down outright unless he's particularly disgusting,' he said and I smiled.

"Who else but my father would think me pretty? I wondered, even in this great dress.

"My father looked like he read my thoughts.

" 'I don't want you underestimating yourself, Cathy. Don't seem surprised and so grateful when a boy asks you to dance. In fact, hesitate for a moment as if you're deciding whether or not he's worthy of you.'

" 'Oh Daddy,' I said. 'I don't think I can do that.'

"After all, I thought, I had never yet been asked to dance by any boy ever. Even if the first looked like Frankenstein, I'd surely say yes quickly.

" 'I want you to make them wonder,' " he said firmly. 'It's important that you establish self-respect in their eyes immediately. Okay,' he continued, 'I'm the one asking you to dance. Look like you're thinking about it. May I have this dance, Cathy?' he pretended. 'Go on. Do what I said. Just a quick glance around as if you're checking to be sure no one else is waiting in the wings. Go on. Do it,' he told me and I pretended too, feeling foolish, but doing what he wanted anyway. 'Good,' he said. 'Now a small smile, a nod and step forward.'

"I did as he told me and he held out his arms. He listened to the music for a moment.

" 'This is one of those dances we can actually dance together,' he said with a laugh. 'I'm sure the nuns won't permit anyone to dance any closer than this,' he said putting his hand on my waist and holding my other hand up. We moved around my room. 'That's good,' he said. 'Fine. However, you should expect some boys might still try to take advantage when the nuns aren't watching so carefully. They'll move you a bit closer like this and their hands may move off your hip like this and slide over your rear end. See,' he said.

" 'What do I do?' I asked quickly.

" 'Step back and then say, "Watch your hands if you want to dance with me." Make sure you say it like you mean it, okay?'

"I nodded. I was very nervous now and worried. Was this all going to happen? How did Daddy know so much? I wondered as well.

" 'Do it,' he said.

"I stepped back. 'Watch your hands if you want to dance with me,' I repeated. He shook his head.

" 'Firmer. Mean it,' he told me and I did it again, trying to sound serious.

" 'Okay. That's better,' he said. 'Good,' he continued.

" 'What if the boy doesn't want to dance with me anymore?'

" 'Good. You've eliminated an idiot.

" 'Now, however, if you get to like one particular boy and he seems to like you, too, he might ask you to sneak out of the dance with him. What are you going to say?'

" 'I don't know,' I said, unable to even imagine such a scenario. 'No, I guess.'

" 'That's what you *should* say.' He held his gaze on me and a small smile formed in the corners of his lips. 'But you might be tempted. He might be a very good looking boy or popular,' he warned, lifting his voice.

" 'I won't do it,' I promised.

" 'Nevertheless, whether it happens at this dance or the next, it will happen someday, Cathy. It's natural no matter what you promise now. You're prettier than you think and boys will be boys. You're going to want to go and I'm not saying you never should. I just want you to be prepared when you do eventually give in to your inner voice,' he said.

" 'Inner voice?'

" 'Every man and every woman has one. It's usually silent, but at the right moment, at the right occasion, it speaks up. It demands to be heard and you can't stop it. In fact, you might not want to,' he said. 'There are things that are going to occur which will make the voice louder, stronger inside you until finally, it's the only voice you hear. You will no longer hear your mother's voice or even mine.

" 'You've got to be prepared for that,' he told me. 'If not, then what your mother said the other day at dinner will happen. You'll get yourself into trouble. You don't want that, do you?'

" 'No, Daddy,' I said.

"I remember it was as if a frightened little bird had somehow gotten caught in my chest. It fluttered about, its wings grazing my heart, my lungs and my ribs. I felt weak. My legs were trembling. Daddy looked so serious, so worried. How dangerous was all this?

" 'Good,' he said. 'Then we'll do something to prevent it, but like everything else, Cathy, we better keep this as our special secret. Your mother just won't understand. She has different ideas about these things, unrealistic ideas, I'm afraid. I'm not trying to get you not to love her, but you know what I mean, don't you?'

" 'Yes, Daddy,' I said.

"He smiled and then he stepped up to me again and turned me around to look into the mirror.

" 'You are not a little girl anymore,' he said. 'You are a real young lady. Your body is armed, loaded, ready to explode, take off, soar. I'm sure you have already felt some of this. I'm sure,' he added with a tiny smile, 'you have already heard the inner voice, especially in dreams. Am I right? Don't be ashamed or afraid to tell me,' he pursued.

" 'Yes,' I said in a whisper. I wasn't really sure what he meant, but I thought that was the answer he expected and needed. He smiled and brought his face closer to mine.

" 'It's all right. Don't be afraid,' he said. His face looked almost as flushed as mine felt.

" 'All right, let's go to lesson number two,' he decided, stepping away. 'Pretend I'm the boy you like, the one you have been hoping would pay attention to you. Now he has and like I said, he tells you to meet him in the hall.

" 'Pretend to go to the girls' room,' he said in a different voice. He even stood differently and smiled differently. 'They won't know the difference, Cathy. C'mon. You go first and I'll follow. Then, instead of going to the girls' room, meet me just outside the school door. We'll go to my car for a little while. No one will even miss us,' he added.

"It was funny playing this game with him, and yet it was also exciting for me, just like I was in a soap opera or something.

"He stepped closer to me, looked to the side as if checking to see if we were being watched, and then slipped his hand into mine and gently played with my fingers for a moment.

" 'C'mon,' he said. 'I want to be alone with you for a while. Everyone's watching us here. We can't really talk and there are so many things I want to tell you, Cathy. Please. Just for a little while, okay?'

"I could hardly speak. I was afraid to say no, and Daddy was right: there was another voice inside me, tiny but there, a voice encouraging me to go, suggesting that it might be a lot more fun.

" 'Don't disappoint me, Cathy. Please,' he pleaded.

" 'What should I do?' I cried in desperation.

"Daddy stared at me so seriously.

" 'Either go or say no,' he said back in his daddy voice. 'What will it be? You want to go, don't you? Don't you?' he pursued.

" 'A little, I guess,' I admitted.

" 'Okay,' he said. 'That's all right. You're being honest. I'd rather that than you pretend otherwise. We'll just have to move faster to the next lesson,' he said and turned for a moment as if he was thinking and planning.

" 'Where can we go? Where can we go to practice and learn?' he asked himself aloud. Then his face brightened and he turned back to me.

" 'I know.'

"He reached out and took my hand and we left my

room. I thought we were going to go downstairs, but he turned and headed toward his and my mother's room.

"I didn't go into my mother and father's room very often. She kept that door closed all the time, too. I really didn't have much reason to go in there. She did all the cleaning in there. I could help only with the downstairs, the living room, den, dining room and kitchen, as well as my own room and the bathrooms, of course.

"I couldn't remember a time when I was in their bedroom just with Daddy. It felt so strange, almost as if I had gone to an unfamiliar place.

" 'Let's see,' he said standing inside the doorway and looking over the room. 'Yes, that's it. My bed will be the car.'

"He changed his posture and his whole demeanor again and then turned back to me with that eerie smile.

" 'Cathy,' he said. 'I knew you would do it. I knew you would come. I knew you liked me just as much as I like you. Maybe it's even more than that. Like is for kids and we're not kids anymore.

" 'It was so crowded and noisy in there anyway, wasn't it? This is better. C'mon. No one will see us in my car,' he added and pulled me toward his bed.

"He pretended to open a car door and slide in.

" 'Backseat has more room,' he told me as he sat on his bed. 'C'mon, get in.' He beckoned and reached for me and I sat on his bed, too.

" 'Close the door, silly,' he said.

" 'What?'

" 'The car door, Cathy. Close it.'

" 'Oh,' I said and even though I felt a little foolish doing it, I pretended to reach out and pull the door closed.

" 'Would you like a cigarette?' he asked me.

" 'A cigarette? No, I don't smoke,' I said.

"He smiled.

" 'That's good,' he said. 'We wouldn't want anything bad to happen to those beautiful lungs of yours, would we? Relax,' he said putting his arm around me and pulling me a little closer to him. 'We don't have those frustrated penguins staring at us now, making us feel like we're doing something dirty.'

"It was so strange to hear Daddy talk like this, but when I looked at him, his face was so different: the way his lips turned up in a strange smile, the glint in his eyes, everything made him look like someone else. Someone scary.

" 'You're very pretty,' he told me. 'You've been keeping it a good secret, but I always thought there was a pretty girl hiding in there,' he said. 'The other girls are so stuck-up and stupid, but you're not. You're a real girl, Cathy, the kind of girl I could like a lot. I mean that. I really do.'

"I admit I loved hearing Daddy say these things. They were words I had dreamed being said to me many times. It was as if Daddy had gotten into my head and listened some nights and overheard that inner voice he spoke of before, the voice that told me I'd do anything just to be loved.

"Suddenly, he kissed me on the neck. It was such an unexpected kiss; I felt weak and anxious at the same time.

" 'You're delicious,' he continued, nibbling on my ear. 'Just as delicious as I had imagined.'

"While he did this, I didn't realize his hand had slipped off my shoulder. Suddenly, I felt the zipper moving down as he kissed me on the neck and then the side of my face, moving over my cheeks. I think I actually got numb all over.

"He got the zipper almost all the way to my waist and then began to slip the straps off my shoulders, nudging my dress along with them. Everything he did surprised me and the shock of it all paralyzed me.

" 'You like me too,' he said. 'Tell me you like me too. C'mon say it. Say it, Cathy,' he chanted.

"I did. I couldn't help doing everything or anything he asked. Was this what really would happen? I wondered.

"He didn't take my new dress all the way down to my waist. As soon as he had it away from my breasts, he turned me to him and kissed me full on the lips. My eyes popped open. His fingers had unfastened my bra and seconds later, he leaned on me until I fell back on the bed. I could barely breathe. I wanted him to stop—it was so embarrassing.

"I think I made some sort of noise of protest and suddenly, he pulled back, sat up and stared down at me. His face and his neck were all red. He looked like he was having difficulty catching his breath.

" 'Okay,' he finally said, back to his daddy voice. 'Let's stop and review everything. What just happened to you?'

" 'I don't know,' I cried. 'It happened so fast!'

" 'Exactly. That's how boys work. They don't ask

permission for each and every touch and kiss. One thing follows another until here you are half naked and onto the next step,' he said.

" 'There's more?'

" 'Yes, much more,' he rattled. He ran his hands through his hair and looked at my mother's bed for a moment. 'Okay,' he said without turning back to me. 'Dress yourself quickly and we'll go over this. The whole point is for you to learn and be prepared.'

"I did what he said and waited. After another long moment, during which his face returned to a more natural shade, he turned back to me.

" 'What mistakes did you make?' he asked.

" 'I don't know,' I said.

" 'You don't know? How can you not know?'

" 'It all happened so fast, Daddy, and I didn't know what you wanted me to do,' I moaned at his angry expression.

" 'All right, all right,' he said calmly. 'First, you got into the car too eagerly. Any boy who saw that would expect you would be cooperative; otherwise, why get into the car?'

" 'To talk, I thought.'

" 'Boys don't really want to talk. Maybe a little afterward, but not at this point. Talk is just a kind of bait to get you to come out to the car. You can come out and you can get into the car, but you should set the rules quickly. As soon as you got into the car and I kissed you, you should make it clear you'll go no farther,' he explained. 'You didn't even put your hand on mine to get me to hesitate or stop. Any boy who saw you behave that way would think he could go faster and farther.

" 'Now,' he continued, 'you have to decide how far you can go without losing control, understand?'

"I nodded.

" 'Good,' he said standing. 'Good.' He glanced quickly at the clock. 'That's all we have time for today. Your mother should be coming home any moment. You better take off the dress and put it back into the box. I'll keep it in the trunk of my car,' he told me.

"We both knew my mother might find it no matter where I tried to hide it.

"I returned to my room and did what he asked. Then he took the box and went out to his car. It was hidden away before my mother returned.

"I felt terribly confused and upset and guilty about everything that had happened, but I knew if she found out what my father was doing for me . . . and to me, there would be hell to pay in my family. Some lies, as you said before, Misty, are necessary," I added and sat back.

Once again, they were all just staring at me. Jade was the first to fill the silence.

"You didn't know you were an adopted child then, so you still thought he was your real father, right?" she asked.

"Yes, that's right."

"Well, didn't you think it was . . ."

"Disgusting?" Star offered.

"Yeah, disgusting," Jade seconded.

"No, not right away," I said. "I didn't know what to think. When he was touching me it made me scared and upset. But I thought he was very nice to want to help me, to care about things like my dress and do what other girls' mothers might do for them. And, the things he was *telling* me about boys was very helpful. My mother would never talk about these sort of feelings. I told you how she reacted to the Barbie doll. It made her sick to even have sex suggested to her.

"Afterward, I told myself that Daddy didn't want anything terrible to happen to me and yet he still wanted me to be a normal girl and have fun like other girls my age, something my mother didn't seem to want.

"No, I didn't hate him then. Not then," I practically whispered as my eyes filled with tears.

"Okay, Cathy," Doctor Marlowe said softly. "It's okay. You and I knew this might be their reaction in the beginning, right? Cathy?"

I turned to her and glared. For a moment I was very angry at her for bringing me here and getting me to tell all these things. Slowly, I felt my blood cool down.

"Cathy?" she said.

"I'm okay," I snapped back at her. I stared down at the floor. "I just thought he didn't want me to become a bad girl," I muttered.

"Why wouldn't she think that?" Misty piped up. "He was always very nice to her and he tried to buy her nice things. He seemed to care more about her than her mother does."

"I'm sorry," Jade said. "I didn't mean to make you feel bad or guilty or anything. I'm sorry."

"Me too," Star said. "It isn't your fault you're here. That's for sure."

I was quiet, thinking.

"Yes, it is," I said. "It's my fault; it's my mother's fault and it's my father's fault."

I looked up at them.

"I wanted to be loved, to be wanted. There were other voices inside me, screaming at me, but I kept them smothered. I thought maybe Daddy would make me a special girl. Maybe I'd become as sophisticated as some of the snobs at my school. Maybe the boys would really like me and maybe I could be the most popular girl there. I'd surprise them all, I thought. With Daddy's help, I'd surprise everyone, even myself.

"Why can't I be beautiful? I'm tired of being a freak and feeling odd and different and hiding myself. I'm tired of being ashamed of who I am and what I look like. Daddy made me feel pretty and mature and he would make me better than them.

" 'Shut up,' I told the voices inside me that told me what we were doing was wrong. 'Keep still and don't dare try to stop me, not now, not ever.'

"Maybe I was bad then. Maybe I was just as bad as he was. I went to sleep that night anxious, and yet excited about the dance and what boys I might meet there."

I looked up at Doctor Marlowe.

"Maybe that's why," I said referring to the big question we had left hanging between us after all my sessions with her to date. "Maybe this is the reason why I don't hate him as much as my mother wants me to hate him, as much as everyone wants me to hate him."

She nodded, a soft smile on her face.

I looked back at the girls.

Yes, I thought, this is good. I'm glad I'm here. I'll go on no matter what I see in their faces and in their eyes.

8

"**A**s usual, by the time I rose and went down to breakfast the next day, my father had already gone to work. I had had very strange dreams all night. They were full of startling colors and strange places and faces. I remember seeing myself walking through a field of multicolored clouds that then floated away to uncover a field where arms and hands appeared to be growing out of the ground like stalks of corn. I twisted and turned, avoiding them. They reached out toward me as if they had eyes as well as fingers and I had to move and spin to avoid being seized.

"I guess I literally turned and twisted in my bed too, because when I woke, I actually ached all over, especially right here in my waist and in the back of my legs," I explained showing them.

"I was afraid my mother would take one look at me that morning, see how upset I was, and fire a slew of sharp questions, but she was occupied with her electric stove. Something was wrong and she was complaining about the way modern appliances simply created more complicated problems.

"Still, I felt strange after what Daddy and I had done, and I probably would have felt even more anxious about it if it wasn't for a conversation I overheard at lunch. Debbie Hartley was talking about her newest boyfriend Alex Lomax, she was complaining about him, actually. Debbie is one of the most popular girls at school. Everyone believes she has had the most experience with boys, so when she says something about dating or some boy, the girls are all glued to her every word as if she was spouting gospel. I was no exception.

"I sat just within listening range and tried to act as if I wasn't interested, but she began by describing how Alex had tricked her into going for a ride in his father's new Cadillac the night before and then parked in some deserted dump, knowing all along that his intention was to get her into the backseat, 'Where,' she said, 'he surprised me by producing a condom!'

"My ears perked up. It was almost the same situation Daddy had envisioned.

" 'He had the nerve to assume that when I told him before I wasn't ready, I meant we didn't have protection,' Debbie declared. 'Of course, he tried everything, telling me how much he cared for me, how he couldn't sleep because I was constantly on his mind. Then he tried kissing me on the neck, nibbling my ear, acting as if I was nothing more than some car engine he was trying to get started.'

" 'What did you do?' Judy Gibson asked her.

" 'I told him if he didn't back off, I'd kick him where he would remember it until his dying day,' she said with fury in her voice. 'Imagine, using as an excuse my saying I wasn't ready. Boys deliberately misunderstand things you say or misinterpret things you do just to get you to do what they want,' she proclaimed. The girls nodded and bobbed their heads simultaneously like puppets on strings.

" 'So you're not going with him to the dance?' Betty Anderson asked her.

" 'Of course I am. He's cute, isn't he? I can handle him. He'll behave now, but you've got to show them who's in control fast or . . .'

" 'Or what?' Judy asked breathlessly.

" 'Or you'll be pushing a baby carriage in the Beverly Center mall,' she predicted.

"All the girls around her nodded again in unison, all wide-eyed. My heart was racing. Daddy was teaching me the right things, I thought. If all these girls, who supposedly were far more experienced with boys than I was, were this vulnerable, what could I expect?"

"I bet that Debbie Hartley was full of jelly beans," Star said. "She was just trying to be a big deal in front of her sheep."

"You think so?" I asked.

"Why else would she put down her boyfriend in front of them like that?"

"Star's right," Jade said. "I know girls like that, too. They are usually making it up to look like they are more experienced. Unless she's just a sex tease, of course, and likes to torment every boy she dates," she added.

"Maybe," Star said, "but I think we're probably right about her anyway."

Misty said nothing, but nodded with a knowing look on her face.

How I wished I was experienced enough to recognize these things as well as they could, I thought.

"Nevertheless, it was on my mind the remainder of the day. I couldn't stop thinking about it all, even when I got home and started my homework. Daddy came home late that night and my mother complained about the stink of booze on his breath. He did look like he had drunk more than usual. His eyes were a little more bloodshot and he had this devil-may-care smile on his face as she chastised and lectured him.

"He didn't say anything special to me, but at dinner, I caught him looking my way occasionally and winking. Of course, I checked to see if my mother had caught us conspiring each time, but she was occupied with the meal and with reminding my father about her great-uncle Willy who had become an alcoholic from his daily drink with the boys and ended up dying in the gutter, penniless. It was one of those family stories that takes on the power of a legend. My father was never very impressed with it and once told her that her mother probably made it all up.

"That set her off on a tirade against his family, whom she called white trash. Daddy never defended them no matter what she said. As I grew older, I wondered why, but he always retreated from my questions with the statement that they were all 'A bunch of lunatics.' According to him, it was better to pretend they didn't exist, that they never existed.

"After dinner my father fell asleep in his chair reading and my mother continued her complaining, only now, directing it to me.

" 'See what a waste of energy it is to get yourself drunk,' she pointed out, nodding in his direction. 'It's better you never put your lips to any alcohol.'

"I thought about what had happened at Kelly's after I had begun to drink the rum and considered that she was probably right about that.

"Anyway, I went up to my room for the night. I heard her go to bed before Daddy and then, after I had bathed and gone to bed myself, I heard his footsteps on the stairs. He paused at my door. I held my breath and then I saw the door open slowly. He slipped in and closed it behind him.

" 'Cathy? Are you asleep?' he whispered.

" 'No, Daddy,' I said. 'I just got into bed.'

" 'Good,' he said and approached the bed. He sat at my feet for a moment. I could hear him breathing hard as if he had run up the stairs. Then he reached out and lay his hand, palm down, on the small of my stomach.

" 'Are you still excited about going to the dance?' he asked.

" 'Yes, Daddy,' I said.

" 'Good,' he said. 'Well then, it's time to go on with our lesson.' He rose to sit closer to me. 'Remember where we were. You like this boy and you want him to like you,' he said quickly. 'Now boys can do something that is so unexpected and surprising to you, you'll get confused and lose your control,' he told me, which was almost exactly what Debbie had told her girlfriends at school.

"I heard what sounded like the rustle of clothing and a moment later, he lifted the cover and slipped into bed beside me.

"When I was a little girl, he had done this once. My mother was busy downstairs and he came into my room and slipped into the bed and held me and stroked my hair and petted me as he talked about things we would do together someday. I used to long for him to be like that again.

" 'Now remember where we were when we left off,' he whispered in my ear. 'You're in the backseat of his car and he has kissed you and told you he loves you and needs you and wants you to love and need him, and you like all that. You want all that. Then he moves quickly,' Daddy said and put his hand where it was on my thigh the day before.

"I held my breath, waiting for him to tell me what I was supposed to do. When he didn't speak, I thought he was waiting for me to move his hand away, but he moved it to that very private place between my legs before I could do anything.

" 'When he touches you here, it's different,' he said. 'It makes that inner voice louder, right?

" 'Oh Cathy,' he said in that pretend voice before I could respond. 'You feel so good.'

"Then, without warning as he had promised, he turned himself and I felt his hardness against my inner thigh. He was right about it surprising me. I couldn't speak; I couldn't move. It was more than just a shock. It turned me to stone.

" 'He'll want you to touch him, Cathy. You should know what it's like for him so you will know what to expect. Here,' he said bringing my hand to him. 'See what happens to him. See?' he said.

"He held my hand there and I felt his heart beating through my palm.

"I cried out and turned away quickly, burying my face in the pillow.

" 'That's all right,' he said. 'That's good. That's the way you should be, but now you know what to expect. That's good, isn't it? Isn't it?' he asked again until I nodded my head. 'Good,' he said. 'Good,' he chanted, but he sounded a little frightened too.

"He rose and I heard him dress and start for the door.

" 'Good night, Cathy,' he said. 'That was tonight's lesson. There's just one more step to go,' he added as he opened the door and slipped out.

"I couldn't stop crying and then I became angry at myself. Why was I crying? Look at what Daddy had done for me. In minutes I was ahead of the other girls who would probably learn all this while it was happening and wouldn't know what to expect. I was more sophisticated than Debbie Hartley. Stop crying. Stop being a baby. Stop being immature, I told myself.

"Damn, Cat, didn't you know how wrong it was?" Star asked.

"I thought it was good!" I protested. "I didn't know. I had no one to talk to about it all. Daddy was nicer to me than ever!" I cried, tears now building aggressively under my eyes and pouring over my lids to streak down to my chin.

"Easy, Cathy," Doctor Marlowe said. "We've talked at length about this. You don't have to be ashamed. You don't have to blame yourself. The girls understand," she added looking at them.

Misty nodded.

"Is he in jail at least?" Jade asked.

"No," I said.

"Why not?" she demanded.

"Let Cathy tell you everything at her own pace, Jade. If she wants to go on, that is," Doctor Marlowe said.

The girls sat back and looked at me anxiously. They didn't look angry so much as they looked frightened now. I was beginning to feel like I was the strongest of us all.

"I'll go on," I said.

Misty leaned forward and touched my hand. She smiled and I took a deep breath.

"Daddy was very busy the next two days. Something dramatic had happened in the stock market and he missed dinner on Wednesday night. On Thursday, however, he surprised both my mother and myself by telling us that he had to go to Santa Barbara to meet with an important client on Friday. He would leave late in the afternoon, so we could go along. He suggested we stay overnight and have dinner at a nice restaurant on the beach.

" 'It's a great town, great stores. You'll have a good time,' he told my mother.

"Of course, she had her expected reaction. Santa Barbara was so close. Why was it necessary to stay overnight in an expensive hotel where strangers slept? It started her off on one of her favorite topics: her theory about why there was so much disease in the world. She believed it was due to travel, to people spreading germs and viruses. She was especially critical of air travel, claiming the germs were circulated for hours and hours in a plane. She had never been in a plane for just that reason, and she would certainly not go to Santa Barbara and stay overnight in some hotel.

" 'Oh, too bad,' Daddy said and then turned to me and asked if I would want to go with him. 'It's a business expense,' he said. 'The client is actually going to pay for it. I can get us a suite.'

"I looked to my mother but she seemed uninterested in my answer. I don't know if she thought I was going to be like her and refuse or if she didn't really care what I decided. Daddy looked at me with eyes that told me he really wanted me along.

" 'We'll be home early enough for you to prepare for the dance,' he added, then looked at my mother and winked at me.

" 'Okay,' I said.

" 'Good,' he said quickly. 'I'll swing by after you come home from school and we'll head out to beat the traffic. Sure you won't join us, Geraldine?'

" 'Of course, I'm sure,' my mother said.

"Didn't she realize what was going on?" Jade asked quickly, her face flaming bright red with fury.

I shook my head.

"It was so far from her thoughts, she couldn't even imagine it," I told her.

"I bet she feels really bad now," Star said.

"She does but she blames him the most, of course," I said. "And me, too."

"Forget about blame. What happened? Did you go with him?" Jade asked.

"Yes. I was very nervous all the next day. The talk at school was all about the dance, of course, and some of the girls were asking me what I was going to wear. When I described the dress my father had bought, they looked envious. It made me more confident and even proud and more appreciative of Daddy.

"When I got home, I packed a small bag for overnight. My mother acted as if she had either forgotten or hadn't paid enough attention to understand I was going. She didn't try to stop me, of course. Why would she?

"All she said was, 'Make sure you take a bath in the morning and wash away all the germs you'll get on you sleeping in someone else's sheets. Wear as much as you can to sleep, too,' she advised.

"I promised I would and a little while later, Daddy arrived to pick me up. Shortly afterward, we were on our way. It was the first time we ever went anywhere alone overnight. I was naturally nervous and excited.

" 'I have a surprise for you,' he said after I got into the car. 'Check the backseat.'

"I saw three boxes from a department store.

" 'What is it, Daddy?'

" 'Look for yourself,' he said with a laugh and I reached over the seat and brought the boxes forward into my lap. First, there was a small box full of cosmetics: lipstick, eye shadow and makeup. Then he had bought me more clothes, clothes my mother would surely forbid. There was a soft pink cotton sweater, a pair of black Capri pants and black square-toe flats.

" 'Oh Daddy,' I said. 'Where can I wear this? Not to school, you know. Mother would be furious.'

" 'No, it's just for today and tonight. We'll keep it all beside your dress in my car trunk for another time. I know what your mother would say, too,' he added, raising his eyebrows. 'But she's just out of touch with things today.' He smiled at me and then leaned over and kissed me on the cheek. 'Go on,' he said, 'climb into the back and put it on.'

" 'Now?'

" 'Sure. Let's arrive in Santa Barbara in style,' he said, laughing.

"I was so excited about it, I did what he suggested. The sweater was a lot tighter than I would have liked and it had a deep, V-neck collar. There was no hiding my bosom in this, I thought, and the pants were tight, too.

" 'I don't really know how to put on makeup, Daddy,' I said, but I put on the lipstick anyway.

" 'That's okay,' he said. 'I wanted you to have it. I want you to have self-confidence, Cathy. Your mother has gone about all this in the wrong way. But we're fixing things,' he added, 'right?'

"I was so thrilled with what was happening, I agreed quickly. When we stopped at a gas station, I hopped out and went to the bathroom to look at myself. I couldn't believe the change. It actually frightened me. Was this really me?

"Daddy looked so pleased. The gas attendant was staring at me hard when I returned to the car.

" 'See that,' Daddy said. 'See the way that young man was ogling you? You are attractive, Cathy. Never think you're not,' he said.

"How good that made me feel. I felt like hugging

him and thanking him. He cared about me. Nothing else seemed to matter for the moment, nothing."

I glanced at Doctor Marlowe. She looked displeased. I could hear her coaching me: Stop trying to explain yourself. Stop trying to find excuses. It wasn't your fault.

Nevertheless, I thought, Mother was right. How could it not have been some of my fault? I still believed that, even now, even as I told the story of what happened that night.

"A little while later, we pulled into the motel. It was right near the ocean.

" 'Where are you meeting your client, Daddy?' I asked him.

" 'I'll call from our room,' he said, 'and see what he wants me to do.'

"The room he got for us wasn't a suite. It was just a room with a king-size bed.

"He saw the surprise in my face when we entered together.

" 'This is the room with the best view,' he said. 'The bed's big enough, right?'

" 'I guess so,' I said hesitantly.

"Never before in my life had I ever slept in a bed with anyone, not even as a child. My mother always made it clear to me that I couldn't come crawling into her bed or my father's. If I was afraid or just needed to be held, I had to smother those feelings.

"Daddy called his client and left me at the motel while he went to see him. There was access to the beach behind the complex and I took off my shoes and walked barefoot in the water as the tide washed ashore.

I kept thinking how Mother would complain that I would track in sand or catch some disease on my feet. It made me laugh and I was suddenly filled with this great sense of freedom. It was as if Daddy had snuck me out of the castle, out from behind the high walls and chains of rules. Here I could soar, laugh, splash and be devil-may-care.

"It was a beautiful afternoon, with just a few wispy clouds across the horizon. I threw myself on the beach and stared up at the blue sky, dreaming of floating up into it. The sand was so warm and cozy. I must have fallen asleep for a while because suddenly I heard Daddy's laugh.

" 'There you are,' he cried. 'I thought you might have run off with that gas station attendant.'

" 'Oh Daddy,' I said. 'He wasn't really looking at me that way.'

" 'Like hell, he wasn't!' Daddy exclaimed. In our house my mother hated when he said hell or damn, not because she was so religious. She just thought it was crude and a bad influence on me. Out here with the vast ocean before us, the wind blowing through my hair, the sky so blue, nothing, no rules, mattered.

" 'Well,' he said, 'I'm free now. What would you like to eat? Why don't we have seafood? We're at the ocean,' he said. Everything sounded exciting to me.

" 'Should I change back into my other clothes?' I asked.

" 'Absolutely not,' he said. 'I want everyone to be jealous of me.'

"He reached down for my hand and we walked back to the motel together, where he showered, shaved and dressed while I watched television. We went to a very nice restaurant on the wharf and I had lobster and then we shared a dessert, something called a mud pie, which was a wedge of vanilla ice cream smothered in hot fudge. Again, I could hear my mother chastising us for eating such a rich dessert.

"Before we returned to the motel, we did what he had promised: we went into the town and visited some of the quaint shops. He bought me some inexpensive but interesting artistic jewelry, a necklace and a ring. He said they would go well with my new party dress, the one he had bought, of course.

"It was one of the happiest and nicest days I could remember. When we returned to the motel, I assumed we were going to sleep. I got ready for bed. Daddy watched television, sitting in a chair, and his eyes closed. I never felt as contented so I was confident that I would have only good dreams.

"Some time after I had fallen asleep, I woke in the dark room because I felt him beside me.

" 'It's time for your last lesson,' he whispered, his lips touching my ear.

"My heart began to pound.

" 'What, Daddy?'

" 'Girls who do go too far are like swimmers who have gone beyond the buoy out in the ocean you saw today. The waves have taken control. Despite what they want now, they are lost in the rhythm and can only wait for it to end.'

"As he spoke to me softly, he ran his hands over me, lifting my nightgown.

" 'Daddy,' I moaned. 'This is wrong!'

" 'You have to know what this is like,' he insisted. 'And it's not wrong. It would only be wrong if I were your *real* daddy.'

"Not my real daddy, I thought. What did he mean? The shock in my eyes made him stop.

" 'You're finally old enough to know the truth, Cathy. Yes, you're adopted, but even though you were adopted, we've always loved you. Still, don't tell your mother I've told you. It was something we were supposed to do together someday. Don't worry about it. You're my special girl, remember.' He moved his body over mine and kept whispering in my ear, 'My special girl. My special girl.'

"It hurt, but I don't know what hurt more: what he was doing or finding out the truth about myself. I was spinning with such confusion, it all seemed like a whirlwind of nightmares. I cried and cried and in the morning, I saw the blood. There was some on my nightgown. He told me I had to throw it away. If I didn't, my mother would wonder and the most important thing, always the most important thing, was keeping our special secret.

"I wasn't very talkative the next morning. For a while, the shock of all that had happened took my attention away from what he had told me. Daddy tried to cheer me up. He talked about other places we would visit, now that I was old enough and could be independent. A few times, I thought I would ask more about my adoption, but I couldn't bring myself to form the words.

"We got back on the highway and headed for home. Again, he tried cheering me up by talking about the dance and how much fun I was going to have. I fell asleep for most of the trip and didn't wake up until we were pulling into our driveway.

" 'Everything all right?' he asked me before we got out.

"Everything all right? I thought. You told me I was adopted and after what we did, everything is supposed to be all right?

" 'Yes,' I lied and hurried into the house.

" 'Did you take your morning bath?' was my mother's first and only question the moment she saw me. She didn't ask a thing about the day, where we had gone or what we had done. I told her yes and went up to my room.

"I looked into my mirror and didn't recognize the girl I saw there. I couldn't shake off the feeling of being dirty. I still feel like that once in a while, but learning I was adopted, that I had a mother and father that I had never known left me feeling even more empty inside. Shattered . . ."

"You can stop now, Cathy," Doctor Marlowe said.

I gazed at her and shook my head.

"No," I said. "I can finish."

She smiled at me.

The three girls, my sister Orphans With Parents, weren't smiling. They were the ones holding their breath now.

I wanted to say, "It's all right. Everything's going to be all right."

But I had no idea if it was or ever would be.

9

"**I** think something died inside me that night at the motel."

I looked at Doctor Marlowe and smiled.

"Some people think it was innocence. The little girl was gone, swept away abruptly.

"I felt so tentative about myself, so uncertain. Rather than my now being armed with a new, mature confidence, I felt like I was blindfolded, walking on a tightrope, unsure about every step, anticipating some great fall. With that feeling came the loss of all the excitement that I had felt building in me about the dance. I wasn't even interested in going anymore. I felt sick, weak, drained of my emotions.

"I lay on my bed and stared up at the ceiling for hours with my eyes wide open, thinking of nothing that I can recall.

"Daddy was the only one to check on me. Mother

128

wasn't doing anything to encourage my going to the dance, of course. When he saw I was just moping about and he realized how late it was, he came up to see why.

"He knocked lightly on my door. I didn't respond and he opened it and peered in.

" 'What are you doing? Don't you have to get ready?' he asked.

"I was afraid to let him know what I was feeling so I complained about being a little nauseous and tired. He came into my room and closed the door behind him.

" 'That's just stage fright,' he said with a smile. 'All girls have it on their first date or social event, Cathy.'

"I didn't agree or disagree. I just turned my head and stared at the pillow.

" 'It's not important anymore,' I muttered.

" 'Not important anymore? Of course, it's important. Cathy, you've got to go now,' he insisted. 'If you don't, your mother will blame it on my taking you to Santa Barbara. She'll start to rant and rave about disease and dirt and all that. We'll never be able to go anywhere again without her bringing it up and complaining. You won't have a minute's peace if you stay home. Believe me.

" 'Besides,' he said, 'I got you that wonderful dress and those shoes and you have the jewelry to wear. You're going to be the belle of the ball. Don't miss this, Cathy. C'mon, sweetheart. Why have I spent all this time with you? All the lessons,' he added. 'After your experience, I'll spend time with you again and we'll talk about what more you need to know, okay? Cathy?'

"I felt my stomach churn and I had to swallow and swallow to keep from having to throw up.

V. C. ANDREWS

" 'Okay, Daddy,' I said. 'I'll start to get ready.'

"I just wanted him away, wanted him to stop talking.

" 'Good. I know just where to pull over between here and the school for you to change into the real dress waiting for you in the car trunk,' he said. 'I'm taking my camera and I'll snap a few shots of you so we can have something precious to remind us of our special secret.'

"He came over and touched my hair and stood there looking down at me. For the first time, I felt myself cringe inside. I was afraid he might sense it, too, but he didn't.

" 'You're so pretty. My special little girl,' he said, leaning down to kiss me on the cheek before he left, closing the door softly behind him.

"It still took a great deal of effort for me to gather enough enthusiasm to bathe, do my hair and dress, but I did. I moved like someone just going through the motions, someone in a daze.

"However, when I put on that dress my mother had bought and insisted I wear, I stared at myself and just started to giggle and giggle. It was like a dam had broken. In fact, I was a lot like I had been at Kelly's house after I had drunk too much rum. I couldn't stop laughing. Tears rolled down my cheeks. My chest and my ribs ached so much, it actually frightened me, but I couldn't stop.

"I tried holding my breath. That didn't work either. My lungs just burst, leaving me gasping for air. My legs gave out and I sat on the bathroom floor. My sitting there with the skirt of that dress all around me oozing green struck me even funnier, I guess, because I laughed hard-

130

er. It was maddening. My peals of laughter were interspersed with dry heaves. My entire insides felt like they were in rebellion. I thought my whole body might come up and out of my mouth, including my lungs and my heart. It would all spill out on the floor."

"Ugh," Misty cried.

"Yes," I said nodding. "My thoughts were disgusting, but I couldn't stop that either. I'm actually leaving out half of it," I told her.

"Forget that. What did you do?" Jade asked. She looked like she understood the madness that had taken control of me, like she'd felt it herself before and she wanted to know how I had handled it. She was leaning forward, practically ready to lunge off her seat at my response.

"I tried to stand by reaching up to the sink and pulling myself to my feet. When my hand slipped off the ceramic, I broke into another fit of hysterics. It was as if the bathroom was coming alive and every part of it, every fixture, was trying to avoid me like I was contaminated or something or maybe, shocked by what I looked like in the 'perfect party dress.'

"My laughter seemed to come from a lower and lower place in my body now. It rolled up in small, thunderous peals, flowing through my throat and echoing in my mouth and my ears. I was on all fours, crawling, and that made me laugh harder. Everything I did, every thought I had, every breath I could take, brought a new surge of hysterics.

"I was afraid it was never going to end. It was like having the hiccups and doing everything possible to stop them, but nothing works, know what I mean?"

They all nodded quickly, especially Jade.

"I crawled up to my bedroom door, the door that was always supposed to be closed. That struck me funny, too: always supposed to be closed. I might die in here before I can get to the door, I thought, but my mother would think that's fine. It was proper.

"I reached the knob and turned it, falling back as I did so. There I was on my back on the bedroom floor, my arms out, looking up at my ceiling again. I was laughing loudly now. My whole body trembled so much, I thought I must be shaking the whole house.

"Yet, neither my father nor my mother heard me. My mother was running the vacuum cleaner downstairs. I turned myself over on my stomach and I crawled out of my bedroom. My laughter stopped for a few moments and I caught my breath and thought it might be over. Whatever it was might be done, but when I reached the top of the stairway and looked down those steps, I started to giggle again.

"I reached out and put my hands down on the next step and then I began to slide, laughing as I did so. My mother must have finally heard something strange. She flipped off the vacuum cleaner and listened and then went into the living room where my father was watching television.

" 'Turn that down,' I heard her say. I was halfway down the stairs on my stomach. He did what she demanded and they both listened.

"Moments later they were at the foot of the stairs, looking up at me, both their faces so twisted and confused by the sight of me, which of course, struck me funny.

" 'What are you doing?' my mother screamed. 'You're ruining your new dress. What are you doing?'

" 'I'm going to the dance, Mother,' I said. I slid down another step or two. 'I know you're not happy about it, but I'm on my way,' I added and I laughed and laughed until I missed a step with my hand and tumbled to my right, over on my shoulder and then my whole body seemed to rise and float as I did a somersault, landing on my back and crying out.

"In seconds I was at their feet. They both looked so surprised and shocked. I wanted to laugh again, but the pain was too sharp.

" 'My God,' my mother said bringing her hand to her mouth, 'what's wrong with her? Is she . . . drunk?'

"She knelt down to smell, twitching her nose like a squirrel. I closed my eyes on her face, choked on a chuckle that was caught in my throat, and passed out.

"When I woke up, I was in an ambulance on my way to the hospital.

"And you know what? I was still wearing that ridiculous party dress," I said. "I guess I babbled quite a bit, revealing enough to draw the paramedic's attention and concern.

"At the hospital emergency room, they put me through some X-rays and examined me before they gave me a sedative. I slept through the remainder of the night and when I woke in the morning, my mother was sitting at my bedside staring out the window. She had her chin resting on her open palm and her elbow against her body. She looked so thoughtful and for a moment, so much younger than she was. Actually," I said glancing at Doctor Marlowe, who knew it all of course, "I didn't recognize her."

"Didn't recognize your own mother?" Misty asked. "Why not?"

"At the time I didn't even recognize myself," I replied.

Misty scrunched her nose and her eyebrows dipped toward each other.

"I don't remember this part well, but my mother does. She knows every moment of it by heart and recites it from time to time, reminding me what I put her through."

"Huh?"

"Let her talk," Jade stammered, her hands clenched into fists and resting on her knees. Misty sat back quickly.

" 'Where am I?' I asked my mother.

"She dropped her hand and turned to me. Her face aged back to where it should be in seconds.

" 'You're in the hospital,' she said. 'You passed out at home. They gave you tests and found nothing wrong with you, but you said things.'

" 'What things?'

" 'I don't know everything exactly, something about lessons, and now you're . . .' She looked around the room. 'You're on the mental health floor. You're here for observation and there will be a doctor, a psychiatrist, and maybe someone else coming to speak to you. It's horrible. It's all just so horrible.'

" 'What is?' I cried.

"She shook her head and sighed deeply. I studied her and tried to remember, but it was as if a thick concrete wall had fallen around my memory.

" 'Who are you?' I finally asked her.

" 'What?' she said stepping back. 'What did you say?'

I looked around the room and then at her.

" 'I don't know why I'm here,' I said.

" 'What are you talking about?' She stared at me. 'What are you doing?' she asked, her voice shrill. 'I'm going to get your father,' she added as if it was some kind of threat.

" 'My father?' I asked, a little frantic. Butterflies had begun to flutter in my chest and I didn't know why.

" 'He's downstairs in the cafeteria. He's having coffee and something to eat. Do you want to tell me why you're acting like this? Do you want to tell me what all this means before these strangers start to ask you questions?'

" 'I don't know,' I said turning away from her. 'I can't remember anything.'

"She stood up and hovered over me for a few moments.

" 'I don't know what's wrong with you. I was going to let you go to the dance. I bought you a dress for it.'

" 'A dress? Yes, I remember a dress.'

" 'It's ruined,' she said. She shook her head. 'What are you doing?'

"I was scrubbing my arms and my breasts, wiping something away.

" 'I don't know,' I said and looked around the room again. 'Am I supposed to be here? What am I supposed to do? Can't you tell me who I am?'

" 'Oh dear,' she said and turned. She looked like she

wanted to flee. At the door she paused to look back at me. 'I don't know why you're doing this,' she repeated and left.

"I just closed my eyes and I fell back to sleep and when I woke again, I was alone in my room.

"I lay there quietly, my mind so full of blanks. I struggled to remember, fought with every letter, every word that flowed through my mind. It was very scary. I felt like everything was just inches from me, but I couldn't reach anything. I felt like I was dangling. There was nothing below and nothing above me.

"Finally, a kind-looking older man in a white lab coat came in with a young nurse at his side. He introduced himself as Doctor Finnigan and the nurse as Mrs. Jenner.

" 'Why am I here?' I asked him. 'I can't remember my name either.'

" 'You've suffered a traumatic experience,' he began. 'From what we can tell, it's not a single, explosive experience. You're not physically hurt in any way, but you've still suffered severely enough to cause a condition of generalized amnesia. These things don't last. Don't worry,' he assured me. 'I would like to try some hypnotism,' he concluded.

" 'Hypnotism? You're going to hypnotize me?'

" 'I think it might help. It won't hurt you in any way,' he promised.

"He did have a very kind face, soft blue eyes and gently curved lips.

"He asked me to concentrate hard on this small disc he took out of his lab coat pocket and began to spin, and then . . .'"

"What?" Misty asked.

"I don't know. I woke up confused again, only this time, I felt as if I was coming out of the darkness into the light. I must have been sleeping because it was much later in the day. Mrs. Jenner was there. She asked me how I was and I said, 'I'm fine.' I told her I was hungry and she laughed and went to get me something to eat.

"Doctor Finnigan returned, too, only I didn't remember him immediately. However, I remembered everything else. It came back to me in waves and waves of pictures and thoughts. He introduced himself again.

" 'Why am I in a hospital?' I asked him.

" 'What do you remember last?' he replied.

" 'I was getting ready for the dance. I . . . was looking at myself in the mirror, I think,' I told him and he smiled and said that was good. I was getting better quickly, which was what he had expected. I asked for my parents and he told me my mother would be coming up to see me any moment.

" 'What about my father?' I asked him.

" 'Do you want to see him?' he asked me. He studied my face carefully.

" 'No,' I said.

"He nodded.

" 'You're going to be all right,' he promised, squeezing my hand.

"Mrs. Jenner brought me my tray of food and as I was eating, my mother arrived. She stood outside in the hallway with the doctor and they talked in very low murmuring voices for a while. I finished eating before she came in. Then Mrs. Jenner took the tray and left Mother and me alone.

"She looked very sick, pale, her eyes bloodshot. I can't remember ever seeing my mother cry. If something bothered her that much, she would go off to be by herself. She stood by my bed now and the tears slipped out of the corners of her eyes like fugitives sneaking down her cheeks.

" 'Horrible,' she muttered. 'It's so horrible. He doesn't deny it.'

" 'What?' I asked her. 'Who?'

"She took a deep breath and shook her head. She seemed to suck her tears back into her eyes, straightened her body, filling her spine with steel again, pulling her shoulders up.

" 'Let's not talk about it now,' she commanded. 'Let's never talk about it.'

"Of course, that was not to be." I gazed at Doctor Marlowe. "Talking about it became very important. We've traveled a long way, right, Doctor Marlowe?"

"A very long way, Cathy."

"Are we home yet?" I asked her. I was trembling a little.

"Almost, honey," she said. She looked at the other three who were sitting quietly. "You're all almost there," she said with a smile.

I nodded and took another deep breath.

"I remained in therapy for a while, working with Doctor Finnigan. By the time I returned home from the hospital, Daddy was gone. Like your mother, Misty," I reminded her, "my mother had tried to purge the house of everything that would remind us of him. She didn't go so far as to sell or give away his favorite chair, but she didn't just clean out his closets and drawers. She sanitized them. She scrubbed the house as if his essence, the very memory of him, was something that could be vacuumed up, scrubbed away.

"Unlike you, Jade, I didn't have to be involved in much of the legal stuff. I knew my mother had started the process of getting a divorce, of course, and I knew that lawyers had met and settlements had been concluded to her satisfaction.

"Like your daddy, Star, mine was gone suddenly, almost as if some wizard had made him disappear. I know it was part of whatever was decided that he would never have any contact with me again. It wasn't something I easily accepted or believed. To this day I sometimes expect him to appear, to come walking up the stairs, to knock on my door and open it and smile at me and ask how his special little girl is doing.

"It would be like everything that has happened was just a bad nightmare.

"But then, my mother is always there to remind me it was no dream." I looked at Doctor Marlowe. "That's good and bad, I know. I have to face the demons to destroy them, to rid myself of them," I recited.

She nodded.

"But it would be nice to bury them forever."

"You will," Doctor Marlowe promised.

"Why wasn't he arrested? Why didn't he go to jail?" Jade wanted to know.

"First, my mother didn't want all the notoriety. Even today, not that many people know the real reason for their separation and divorce. Second, I don't think I could stand having to tell this story in a courtroom, even if it was only before a judge.

"I did meet with a judge and a representative of a child protection service to conclude custody questions. For a while I thought they might take me away from Mother, too, that maybe they thought she was really more directly responsible. I suppose it was hard for them to believe she was so . . ."

"Dumb?" Star asked.

"Blind," I corrected. "Mother is comfortable in her own world."

"You might as well be away from her," Star muttered.

"I can't say I don't love her or need her. She's the only mother I've ever known."

"I still don't understand why she wanted to adopt you in the first place," Jade said.

"I know. That's something I have yet to learn. There's much I have yet to learn. She's suggested to me that there were rumors about my father and his sister and maybe that was why his family was so distant. She never talked about it before because it was too disgusting to even form such words with her lips, much less utter them."

"Why would she marry someone like that?" Misty asked.

"I don't think she knew about the rumors before she got married," I said. "It's like I'm just learning about my own family now, like doors are being opened to rooms I never knew existed. I'm unraveling a roll of secrets almost daily. Some of it I want to know, and some I wish I never knew."

Jade nodded.

"My mother was always reluctant to talk about any

of this, as you know. Lately, I think she has realized her own need to get stuff out, although it's still not easy to get her to do it. I think she's also afraid of what it might do to me. To her credit, I think she wants me to get stronger and stronger, but she wants it to be something we keep in our own house, in our own world."

I sat back and suddenly, I felt so tired I couldn't keep my eyes open.

"Well," Doctor Marlowe said. "I think we should stop. We've gone about as far as or actually even further than I had hoped we would."

"I guess we can each stop feeling so sorry for ourselves," Jade said. "Is that it?"

"In a way. The most important thing is none of you should feel alone, lost, so different you think you are the only one who has been singled out for what happened in your lives. There are other people, many people who will understand.

"Each of you is special. Each of you have a great deal to recommend you and to make you feel good about yourselves. You're all attractive, intelligent young women and you will overcome all of this difficult and sad history."

"Thanks to you," Misty said.

"No," Doctor Marlowe said looking at all of us, "thanks to yourselves. I'll be seeing each of you again, separately, but I don't think we're going to have to go on and on much longer. You've all made very significant progress. You've made the big turn," she said, smiling.

She glanced out the window.

"Look, the sun's breaking out. Jade, you can get

back to that summer vacation you're supposed to be enjoying."

"Right," she said. Then she smiled and nodded. "Right."

Doctor Marlowe stood up and we all rose. We could hear music coming from upstairs, something from an opera.

"I've heard this in the school music suite," Misty said. "Isn't it *Gianni Schicchi?*"

"Yes, very good, Misty," Doctor Marlowe confirmed.

"I'll get you tickets to our school concerts this year," Misty told her. "It's not quite the opera, but it's close!"

"Thank you. Emma would like that. Good-bye, girls. Have a good week. Until I see you all again," she added and reached out for each of us to squeeze our hands.

When we opened the front door, we could see that today my mother was the first one who had arrived. She sat impatiently, nervously. Her eyes darted toward us and then away. I could almost see her knuckles turning white as she clutched the steering wheel.

All three looked at her. Then Jade turned to Star.

"I guess it isn't easy for anybody," she said. Star offered a reluctant grunt of agreement.

Doctor Marlowe closed the door behind us.

"Anybody want my phone number?" Misty asked.

"I'll just take everyone's," Jade said. She smiled at Star's look of surprise. "I'm the president of the OWP's. I'll call you all when it's time for us to have our first real meeting. Maybe I'll have a brunch or something."

She gave us her number. My mother kept giving me looks.

"I've go to go," I said. "Thanks for being good listeners."

"I guess we can all say that to each other," Misty said.

"You've got that right," Star added.

Jade fixed her eyes on my mother again and then suddenly, she started ahead of me, toward my mother's car.

"What's she doing?" Star asked but followed. We all did.

Oh no, I thought, if she says something horrible . . .

"Hi, Mrs. Carson," she said. "You've got a very nice daughter. Have a nice day," she added. Then she threw me a sly smile and sauntered toward her limousine.

"That girl," Star said muttering. She looked at my mother. "Hello," she said. "She's right. See you, Cat," she told me and started for her grandmother's car.

"Bye," Misty said to me. "We'll see each other again. I'll bug Jade until she does what she promised."

"Okay."

"Hi," she sang toward my mother and waved. Then she hurried toward the waiting taxicab.

I opened the car door and got in.

"What was that all about?" my mother asked, a look of astonishment on her face.

"I don't know. Nothing much, I guess," I said.

"How did it go in there?"

"All right."

"Aren't you going to tell me anything?"

She still hadn't started away.

143

"There isn't anything you don't know, Mother. The question is, are you going to tell *me* everything?" I asked.

She fixed her eyes on me while they grew small for a moment and then she nodded and we drove away, the others right behind us, like a parade or maybe . . . a funeral.

After all, we had buried enough sadness to fill a good-size cemetery.

Epilogue

Mother and I didn't talk about anything significant for a few days afterward. I understood that like me, Mother was trying to find her way through all this. Sometimes, it seemed as if tall weeds and vines had grown from the floors and ceilings in our house and we were hacking our way through to reach each other. I remembered how much importance Doctor Marlowe placed on patience and understanding. I, of all people, knew how bad it was to force someone to open the doors to dark rooms.

Mother attacked her housework and all her chores with a vengeance, searching for something to fill every waking moment so she wouldn't have to stop and think and remember.

It was hardest during our meals. When she finally had everything on the table and we had nothing left to do but sit and eat, there would be that terrible, deep silence. If I looked at her, she would start to rattle off orders, telling me about things she wanted done in the house and then quickly following that with a list of things she needed to do herself.

"He wasn't all that much help around here," she muttered one night. "I had to do most everything that concerned this house myself anyway."

That was her first reference to my father since I had returned from the final group therapy session at Doctor Marlowe's. I offered to be of greater help to her and she promised she would give me more to do. She thought I could handle more responsibility.

She definitely needed more help. Every once in a while, I would notice her stop whatever she was doing, place her hand against her chest and close her eyes. She looked like she was waiting for her heart to start beating again.

"Are you all right, Mother?" I asked.

She hesitated, took a breath and nodded.

"I'm fine," she said. "As fine as I could be under the circumstances."

"Maybe you're working too hard, Mother," I said.

"I'm fine," she insisted and walked away quickly.

Finally, one night I came downstairs and found her sitting in the living room, gazing out the window. She was in the rocker and she was moving herself back and forth gently. I could see she was so deep in thought, she didn't even realize I had entered the room. I sat across from her and waited. Her eyes moved very slowly until she saw me and then they widened and brightened.

"How long have you been there?" she asked.

"Just a few seconds," I said.

"I didn't hear you come in." She sighed. "Looks like it might rain again. I think we're getting a leak in the roof over the pantry. I'll have someone check it tomorrow."

"Mother, there was a question that kept coming up in my group therapy."

"What question?" she fired at me.

"A question I have had in my own mind for a while now. I don't want you to get angry at me for asking it, but it's important to me."

"I hate questions," she muttered. "Ever since what happened happened, that's all the world's been full of for us, questions."

"People have to have answers, Mother. I need answers just like anyone."

"Answers can make for unnecessary trouble. Sometimes it's best not to ask questions," she said.

"No, Mother," I pursued. "It's never better to bury your head in the sand."

"Is that what that doctor taught you?"

"No. I taught it to myself. If I had asked some questions and if you had . . ."

"All right," she said. "All right. Let's get this over with. What question?"

I paused and she looked away as if to make it easier for me.

"Why did you adopt me?"

"What?" She turned back to me. "What kind of a silly question is that?"

"It's not a silly question, Mother. Was it because

you lost a child and didn't want to try to have another?"

"What? Who told you I lost a child?"

"Daddy."

"It was another one of his lies. He was just trying to get you to feel sorry for him and blame me for everything wrong in this house."

"That wasn't true?"

"No."

"I thought it was. Being a mother has never been easy for you, and I couldn't help feeling that all the time."

"Blaming me. I knew it."

"I'm not blaming you. I'm asking you to be honest with me. I need to know everything. I'm old enough now, Mother. I've been forced to grow up quickly," I added.

She glanced my way, her eyes filling with pain.

"Why does everything have to be explained all the time?"

"I have a right to know about myself, Mother. I'll never get better if you don't help me. It might even help you," I added.

She stared at me, looked out the window and rocked. I didn't think she would say any more. I expected I would just go upstairs and leave her in silence as I had done so many times before.

"My mother," she said suddenly, "got pregnant at forty-four. It was a very big surprise to my father." She looked at me.

I was afraid to speak, afraid she might stop.

"Soon after she announced she was pregnant,

your father came into our lives. He was always a sly one, looking for some opportunity. My father was just as sly in some ways. He drew him in like a spider, giving him bigger and bigger investments to handle.

"Howard proposed to me and my father . . . my father came to me and practically begged me to marry him. My mother left for a while and gave birth to you and Howard and I adopted you," she said quickly. "I guess it was all part of the deal. I guess you could say my father sold you and me to Howard in a neat little inheritance-wrapped package. And don't think your father didn't throw that back at me when this all happened," she added with fury in her eyes. "He threatened to tell everyone about your birth, our marriage. It was pure blackmail. Otherwise, I would have seen him put in some jail cell and had the key thrown away."

"My grandmother was really my mother?" I asked incredulously.

She spun on me.

"You wanted to know everything. Now you know. You see why God told Adam and Eve not to eat of the Tree of Knowledge? Sometimes, you're better off in ignorance."

I stared at her.

"We're . . . sisters? Is that what you're telling me?"

She took a deep breath and looked out the window again.

"Half-sisters. Toward the end of his days, my father told me he was convinced he wasn't your father."

"Who is my father?"

"I don't know," she replied quickly, almost too quickly.

She turned to me.

"So now you know all this. Are you going to be better for it? What are you going to do with the knowledge, Cathy?"

"I don't know. It will take time to digest it," I said, swallowing hard.

"You want my advice? Bury it. That's what I did."

"Did you? Did you really ever bury it or did you let it bury you?"

She studied me and then her eyes narrowed.

"So, what are you going to do now? Are you going to hate me more for keeping the truth from you?"

"I don't hate you," I said.

"Are you still going to call me Mother?"

"I don't know how I can start doing otherwise," I said.

She nodded. Then she turned and looked out the window.

"I'm tired, Cathy," she said. "Let's let each other rest," she pleaded.

"Okay," I said and left her rocking, staring into the night, staring back through her own troubled memories.

Her revelations didn't make me feel any better. In fact, they made me feel even more alone, even more like someone just drifting. What did I have to look forward to now? I wondered.

I thought about the other girls. They were like me that way, too. They were drifting.

Maybe we would get together someday.

Maybe we *could* all be friends.

Would that be so crazy?

"No," the lost little girl inside me cried. "It would be wonderful.

"It would be like a few wildflowers who found their way into their own private garden."

V.C. ANDREWS®

All she wanted was to be someone's little girl....
Fate made her a lonely orphan, yearning for the
embrace of a real family and a loving home. But a
golden chance at a new life may not be enough to
escape the dark secrets of her past...

DON'T MISS ANY OF THE FOUR NOVELS
IN THE ORPHAN SERIES

Butterfly
Crystal
Brooke
Raven

POCKET
BOOKS

1462-02

The Phenomenal
V.C. ANDREWS®

V.C. ANDREWS®

LOOK FOR THE THRILLING
CONCLUSION TO THE
WILDFLOWERS SERIES

INTO THE GARDEN

**Coming in December 1999
From Pocket Books**

POCKET
BOOKS

2129